RULES OF ORDER

A NOVEL

JEFF VANDE ZANDE

First Montag Press E-Book and Paperback Original Edition July 2022

Montag Press ISBN: 978-1-957010-13-7
Design © 2022 Amit Dey

Montag Press Team:

Front Cover Artwork: "Mine" by Andrew Rieder
Editor: Charlie Franco
Managing Director: Charlie Franco

A Montag Press Book
www.montagpress.com
Montag Press
777 Morton Street, Unit B
San Francisco CA 94129 USA

Printed & Digitally Originated in the United States of America
10 9 8 7 6 5 4 3 2 1

"Vande Zande creates a world that is tangible, bizarre, and too close for comfort. With a rich, clear voice, he leads us through a place that is at once a home and a constant source of conflict, showing us the different ways its inhabitants contribute to its destruction. *Rules of Order* is a haunting metaphor for our current times, where we are perched precariously on the precipice of complete devastation."

—Jesi Bender,
author of *Dangerous Women* and *Kinderkrankenhaus*

"In this excellent novel of speculative fiction, Jeff Vande Zande reveals a clarity and depth of understanding of our current world and the world to come that one seldom sees but always seeks. He writes with grace and brilliance and a sense of dark humor that suggests he has the gift that Don Delillo and J G Ballard and all of the great writers of speculative fiction have."

— John Guzlowski,
author of *Echoes of Tattered Tongues* and
the winner of the Eric Hoffer/Montaigne Award

"*Rules of Order* is a fresh and welcome take on the dystopian novel. Within one story, one building, Vande Zande manages to go beyond what is expected, bringing together elements of mystery, romance, action, environmental awareness, and political intrigue, all told with a clean and effortless prose that keeps the pages turning. This book is a call to action, with a protagonist worth cheering for, and readers who want to be shook from their slumber would be well advised to take the ride."

— Pete Stevens, author of *Tomorrow Music*

DEDICATION

This book is dedicated to all the activists out there… those who look at the troubles of the world and say, "It doesn't have to be this way." It's for those who follow their words with actions.

ACKNOWLEDGMENT

I would like to thank Skip Renker and Dave Larsen for being early readers of *Rules of Order*. Their positive reaction to what I'd written gave me the confidence to engage in the long editing and rewriting process.

CHAPTER 1

Harvey Crowe blinked his eyes open into the dim light of his bedroom. More often than not, it was nightmares that woke him lately—prophetic hallucinations of the impending collapse. Black and white visions from his subconscious haunted his deepest sleep. They were images he fought to keep at bay during his waking hours. If he didn't, they could leave him nearly paralyzed for hours.

In the dreams, the towering building he lived in—they all lived in—stood momentarily but then, as if pressed from above by a giant, invisible hand, it began to disintegrate. The unseen palm pushed as though on a collapsible telescope, but with such determined force as to drive the lenses shattering into each other. Plumes of debris spread outward from random floors, like the rings of a planet. And then the building was gone… nothing but dust and death dissolving into the gray, lifeless landscape around it.

But he recalled no such dream. He wasn't entangled in chilled, sweat-soaked sheets. His heartbeat and breathing were normal. None of the metallic taste of adrenaline coated the inside of his mouth.

No, something else had woken him.

The building's pipes hummed in the walls and echoed with the sound of water and waste moving up and down the multitude of copper and PVC lengths. A loud groan signaled what the building's Board of Directors had come to call a 'Settling Sequence.' "Harmless," they said, not unlike when people get older and lose height, a natural consequence of aging. "Good bones," they said. The building has good bones.

The thump and churn of water in the pipes, the haunted moans of the building settling… his sleep had been soundtracked by them for so long that he knew that's not what had awoken him. It couldn't have been. They were like white noise to him. Even distant shouting in the hallway or the screams of an assault hardly made him stir. Not for indifference but for familiarity.

On his wall, a reflection from the dim night light's glow highlighted the reinforcing epoxy that filled a five-foot-long crack in the concrete. He could see where the fissure was growing several inches past the epoxy's reach. Cracks had become so epidemic that for the last six months members of the maintenance crew could be seen lugging huge caulking guns and pounding on the doors of the lower floors. The expense had become enough for the Board to implement an Epoxy Tithe. The new tax fell on tenants who lived on the 20th floor and lower. Reassuring letters from the Board explained that, more than a filler, the epoxy once fully cured, was stronger than the concrete, like that of a healed broken bone.

Crowe's mother had worked as a nurse in the building's sublevel infirmary. She'd told him that the idea of a fractured bone healing stronger than before was just a myth. "It's true," she'd said, "that a cuff of strong new bone forms around the break site to protect it. So, for a short time, the fracture is stronger, but the cuff goes away over time. Then you just get regular old bone."

He smiled into the darkness, remembering this. His mother had always taken the time to explain the world to him. As an only child, he was treated by his mother and father almost as a third adult in their home, even from a young age. They didn't talk in code around him, and when he asked questions, they gave honest answers. Being raised that way had not made for an easy childhood when his school years started. To him, his peers lacked curiosity and seemed woefully uninformed. To them, he was a know-it-all and the teacher's pet.

His mind went to Dagmar, and he wondered what she would have thought of him in his school days. She probably would have bullied him too. And now, somehow, they were aligned as members of a group set on saving the fate of the building. She was by far the most militant member with ideas that scared him. One of Dagmar's experts had looked into the claims about the epoxy, and they too were dishonest, he determined. "More goddamn lies from the Board," Dagmar had said, throwing a knife that stuck into the baseboard of Crowe's kitchen.

He winced at the memory of her anger. Her combat boots. Her sneer.

Her lips. Her passion. Her lithe body.

Stop it, he thought.

Her language, more and more, suggested that drastic measures were needed, even if it meant violence. He couldn't let his loneliness keep him from seeing the danger she could be to the cause. She could ruin everything if he let his guard down.

"Waiting for the other shoe to drop… that's all this is," she'd hissed. "Except it won't be a shoe."

Sparked by an impulse, a desire for words, something in the face of Dagmar's ominous ranting, Crowe had told her the history of the old saying.

"What saying?"

"Waiting for the other shoe to drop," he said. "In tenement buildings in New York, the construction was so shoddy, people could hear the slightest movements of their neighbors." Her face registered little interest. "The bedrooms were built one above the other."

"So?"

"At night," he continued, "people would sit on the edge of their beds, unlacing their shoes. Removing one, they'd let it drop to the floor, startling awake their neighbor below." He studied her short-spiked hair, wondering if it could puncture his palm.

Dagmar bent forward to retrieve her knife from the baseboard.

"Are you listening?" he asked.

"Yes," she said, taking her seat again. She ran the tip of her blade under a fingernail. "Just hurry up with your story."

"That's it. The neighbor below would lie awake, staring up at the darkened ceiling, unable to go back to sleep… waiting—"

"For the other shoe to drop. I get it," she said. "Fascinating, Crowe."

He looked at the floor, then up at her again. "It's a metaphor, too. The way we are all connected. The way our thoughtless actions can ripple into the lives of others. The way—"

"That's your problem," she'd said, standing and sheathing her knife. "I mean, you're good… you're good with words. Your newsletter, talking to people on the upper floors… it's a gift. But your belief in words feels naive. Stories. Speeches. Electronic posts. Sometimes they aren't enough." She walked to his door, opened it, and before it fully closed behind her, said, "And when their usefulness has ended, then it's time for action." The last he saw of her was of the sheath strapped to her belt.

The sound of the latch clicking into the strike plate echoed in the room long after she'd left, as though some bigger door had closed.

Crowe threw off his blanket and turned on his lamp. He sat on his bed in the yellowed light. He thought of Dagmar more than he wanted to. She was the closest thing to female companionship he'd known in years. Proximity to her had grown into fondness, even if she was different from him, angry and fierce. He would force himself to remember that she was the de facto leader of the Anti-Collapse Trust or ACT, and the cause worked best if he kept his thoughts for her professional. Plus, he was going to have to keep his wits around her if he was going to be able to temper her rage.

Startling him, the voices of the building's superintendent and his wife echoed in a nearby vent. He shook his head, guessing that maybe it was their bickering that had woken him. By some cruel twist of duct work, his bedroom vent was like a phone receiver eavesdropping on their heated exchanges in the basement-level apartment that they occupied together.

"Anya, that's it, I'm putting tape down the middle of the living room," the super yelled up through the vent's tinny resonance. "The kitchen and bathroom will be neutral territory. Otherwise, you stay on your side."

Crowe rolled his eyes. It sounded like something from a bad comedy he'd once seen.

"I hate you," she yelled back. "All you've ever done is lie to me. From the beginning, you are the worst thing that ever happened to me."

"Venom! That's all you have, woman. You're like a snake."

Crowe went to his bathroom. Standing in front of the mirror, propping himself with his palms against the edge of the sink, he examined his bloodshot eyes and ashen skin. He was too young for so much gray hair. How long had it been since he'd had a full night's sleep? Eaten a decent meal? Did anything other than worry about the fate of the building? Days had become years. And yet what if anything had changed? Most tenants carried on as though nothing were happening.

He grabbed a towel from the metal rack that dangled from loose drywall anchors. Back in the bedroom, he covered the vent with the towel, muffling the arguing coming from the super's apartment.

He fell into bed again, feeling the exhaustion of another fruitless day on the upper floors, knocking on doors, imploring tenants to consider the weight of their things. There were rumors of new hot tubs, gas fireplaces with stone mantles, and new deep freezers. Few cared to listen to him. Some slammed their doors. Others opened their doors only as wide as their chain locks would allow. They admitted to having heard the rumors and load warnings too, but what could be done? Others confronted him. They'd earned their money and it was their right to spend it however they wanted. They didn't want to hear about the size of the cracks in the lower-level apartments. Air pockets, they countered, when he explained that one part of the building had sunk two inches in six years. "Buildings settle into soft soil. It's perfectly natural." It was as though they had memorized the Board's letters of assurance.

Predictions of a complete building collapse made most laugh or shake their heads. Doom and gloom, they said, pointing out their frosted windows towards the hazy shadow of the building's buttressing exoskeleton. They spoke confidently of the Board's plan to install twenty new steel pilings to brace the foundation. For most of the day, the pilings were the biggest counterargument he heard. Twenty new steel pilings! The Board planned to move on Operation Steel in the next few weeks. After that there would be nothing to worry about, they said. Sometimes, standing in a tenant's doorway, he felt even himself being convinced of the foresight and wisdom of the Board.

He tried to counter with the arguments that he and Dagmar had laid out. The foundation had never been constructed for so many residents, their excessive belongings, or the addition of more floors. His arguments felt worn and out-of-date compared to the progressive talk of the steel pilings. A handful of tenants did listen and admitted their doubts about the pilings or anything to do with the Board's promises. "I don't trust Burke," they said of the Board's chairman. Crowe gave such tenants his name and his phone number in addition to his pamphlets, which also included his contact information.

He snapped open his dozing eyes to a blaring sound. After a moment, the telephone rang a second time. His thoughts immediately went to his parents – something wrong with his mother or father. Then, as he always did, he remembered that they had both passed away two years ago. A gas line had fractured in their apartment, asphyxiating both of them in their sleep. The Board's Tenant Liaison member had called him with the news and condolences, naming it an "unfortunate and unforeseeable accident."

Dagmar had approached him then, explaining that the building had experienced a load-related shift that had cracked the gas line. "Your parents are dead due to negligence and greed-induced blindness," she had said to him. Then she'd said more, all of it related to the inevitable collapse of the building. For Crowe, their meeting was an awakening. He quit his job writing marketing copy for Just Like Water and soon after joined ACT and their efforts to save the building. As his parents' only child, he was the beneficiary of a meager life insurance policy that allowed him to eke out a subsistence living while messaging for the cause.

He picked up the ringing phone receiver. Even its lightness felt like a brick in his hand.

"Hello?"

For a moment, he only heard labored breathing coming through the small speaker against his ear. Then: "Can you help me?" a voice asked, old and raspy.

"What?"

"I fell trying to get water. I can't get off the floor."

Crowe sat up. "Why are you calling me?"

"Your number was on a flier under my door."

He rubbed his itchy eyes. "We're just trying to inform tenants—"

"Can you help me?"

Crowe lingered for a moment with the cold of the phone against his ear. "I'm tired. Isn't there anybody else you could call?"

The voice sounded ready to crack into sobbing. "I don't have anybody else. Just my aide, but she won't come again for two days. I'd call her, but the agency doesn't share the aides' phone numbers." He explained that the agency line itself went directly to an automated answering service.

Crowe listened to his stomach rumbling from having skipped both lunch and dinner.

"It's okay," the voice said. "I'll be okay."

"No," Crowe said. "I'll come. What apartment?"

The man gave him a room number nine floors above him.

He exhaled. His thighs ached from the flights he'd been up and down earlier in the day. "Just give me a few minutes."

The deadened voices of the super and his wife continued their endless squabbling under the towel.

"I'll slide the key under the door," the voice said.

Crowe imagined the frail body belonging to the voice lying on a doormat, shivering, waiting for his arrival. "I'm on my way," he said, hanging up.

He quickly dressed and stepped out into the flickering, dim light of the hallway. The smell of cooked cabbage filled his nostrils. In the darker sections, where the sconces were burned out, he felt his hand along the wall. Peeling paint fell to the floor in his wake. He couldn't remember how many work orders he'd sent to the maintenance department regarding the lighting on his floor. Each request was met with a reminder that the Board had made Operation Epoxy a priority over all other maintenance issues. After which, his request would be addressed in the order in which it was received.

Crowe pressed his shoulder into the rusty fire door at the end of the hallway that led into the stairwell. Because they'd stopped working years ago, the locksets and latch sets had been removed. The door swung open easily and then closed itself again behind him. He started up the stairwell counting the floors as he went, his legs burning. At least there were no security gates on the lower landings to deal with. When he was two flights from his destination, he saw a silhouette descending toward him.

"I don't have anything of value," Crowe said as naturally as saying hello.

"That's fine, I don't want anything."

He recognized the deep voice as belonging to Gerald LaMark, one of the newest and youngest board members. Crowe had watched the open board meeting when LaMark had been voted in and confirmed. Where most members of the Board focused their public speeches on the desires of those on the upper floors, LaMark had seemed to be trying to address the needs of everyone. He had his concerns about the building's living conditions on the lower floors. Rumor had it that he was not popular with the older board members and was likely to be voted out in the next cycle. They would run a candidate against him aggressively.

"Director LaMark?"

The trim silhouette stopped on the landing several steps above. Crowe continued until he stood on the landing next to him.

"What are you doing down here, sir?"

LaMark's face was a Rorschach of shadows in the flickering glow of the landing's light fixture. "Just taking a look. I've been told that sometimes what I'm being told about the condition of the lower floors isn't entirely true."

Crowe smiled and nodded. "It's late, though, sir."

"Insomnia."

"I see."

"How?" LaMark asked, smiling. "In this light?"

Crowe confirmed that lighting had been an issue for some time.

LaMark crossed his arms. "Well, you know me. Who are you?"

Crowe reached out to shake his hand. "Harvey Crowe. I'm with the Anti-Collapse Trust," he said, but then immediately wished he hadn't.

LaMark bristled and then walked past Crowe's extended hand. "Well, a good evening then." He stepped down the stairs toward the next landing, his silhouette blending into the darkness.

"Sir?"

LaMark turned, pointing a finger at Crowe. "I'm already seen as a fly in the ointment, Crowe. It wouldn't do for me to be seen talking to a thug."

"A thug? Sir—"

"Confronting delivery people in the hallways? The shoving? Shouting threats at tenants? No, I won't be seen with you. I have work to do. Real work. Good evening." He turned and disappeared in the blackness of the stairs below.

A cold sweat beaded Crowe's forehead. "But I haven't done any of those things!"

LaMark's voice echoed up the stairwell. "If you belong to a group, you are as bad as the actions of the least disciplined member—" The rest of what he said cut out in the closing of a fire door some three or four flights below.

A chill shivered down Crowe's body. "Be careful, sir," he called down into the darkness.

He leaned against the wall. Damn it, Dagmar. She and the others were going further almost every week. Theirs was supposed to be a campaign of information… of truth. Simply inform tenants of the consequences of ignoring the unenforced load infractions. Change the narrative of the half-truths and outright fabrications of the Board. Provide evidence from experts about the instability of the exoskeleton, the band-aid effectiveness of the epoxy, and the longshot possibilities of a successful Operation Steel. Edit and publish STORIES, their newsletter, Crowe's passion project, to make a pipeline of truth available for understanding the actual structural conditions of the building. Work on the minds and hearts of the very people affected by the negligence and ignorance of the Board.

Confronting delivery people? Protesting directly to tenants? It was exactly the direction he feared that ACT would take under the leadership of Dagmar.

He trudged up the remaining flights, feeling none of the fatigue in his legs – his brain on fire. Why would she do this?

When he found and opened the door to the old man's apartment, Crowe spotted him with the doormat draped over his shivering torso, his body a yellowish hue… some sickness wicking to the surface.

"You're here," he murmured as Crowe picked him up and carried him through the hardly furnished living room to the bedroom, his thin arms wrapped around Crowe's neck, the skin of his forearms dry and cold. Crowe's fingers slipped into the pockets between the old man's ribs. He couldn't have weighed more than 100 pounds.

"Thank you," he whispered. "I wasn't sure you'd come."

Crowe set him on the rickety bed and pulled the blankets up over him. Patchy sprouting of a beard grew from his sallow cheeks, the crown of his head overgrown with a thinned shock of white, greasy hair.

He smiled weakly. "I'm a sight, aren't I?"

Crowe touched the old man's frail shoulder. "You're fine. Just fine." He smiled, looking into the pale blue eyes. "Let me get you that water."

He stayed at the faucet with one of the two glasses that he'd found in the cupboard, dumping out the cloudy water again and again. He let the faucet run for a minute and was able to get a glassful that was only slightly discolored.

He handed the glass to the old man who drank it dry.

"More?"

"No, this is good."

Crowe took the glass, filled it again, and set it on the bedside table. "In case you get thirsty later."

The old man thanked him, covering his hand over his yellowing teeth. Reaching up, he smoothed his thin fingers over his head in an attempt to press his wild hair into place.

Crowe watched his self-consciousness. "What does your aide even do?"

"She checks my medications, takes vitals… it's all I can afford."

"How do you—"

"I have a walker," he said, pointing to it in the corner. "I was just stubborn. I wanted to see if I could get to the kitchen and back on my own. Stupid, really. Just… a man wants a little dignity sometimes at this age. Something." He said he wouldn't do it again. "Walker or no, I get dizzy if I stand too long."

Crowe crossed his arms. "You have no family?"

He shook his head. "Never married. Never had children."

Crowe wondered if he was getting a preview of his old age. "I'll be right back. Are you sleepy?"

The man shook his head. "No, I'll be up for a while yet."

Crowe descended back to his apartment and returned fifteen minutes later. Taking a pot filled with warm water from the old man's kitchen, he went back into the bedroom and draped a towel around his neck and shoulders. "Barbershop treatment," he said.

The old man smiled. "I'm game."

Working carefully, Crowe used a dishrag to wet the white hair and then lathered it lightly with shampoo before rinsing it out with the rag. Pulling strands up between his fingers and snipping with scissors, he took two inches off and then combed the hair back over the age-spotted scalp. When he finished, he collected two handfuls of the trimmings, like thatch, and dropped them fluttering into the room's garbage can.

"Let me see the mirror."

Crowe smiled. “Hold on, I’m not finished yet.”

He sprayed shaving cream into his palm and then spread it over the cheeks, under the nose, and over the chin. Soon after, he began to shave him slowly and carefully with a disposable razor, swishing it clean in the pot of water after each stroke.

“I’m Leo.”

“Hmm?”

“My name is Leo.”

He smiled. “Harvey Crowe. It’s a pleasure to meet you, Leo.” He lifted the towel from his thin shoulders and rubbed away the residue of the shaving cream.

“Can you refill that pot with warm water?” Leo asked.

He nodded. When he returned from the kitchen, Leo was looking at himself in the handheld mirror Crowe had brought up with him.

“I look okay.”

“You do indeed.”

Leo put the dishrag into the warm water and then rubbed it into each of his armpits and across his chest protruding with ribs. “I feel ready.”

Crowe smiled. “Not bad treatment from a thug, right?”

Leo set the rag back into the browned water. “Excuse me?”

“Nothing,” he said, shaking his head. He smiled. “You look dignified.”

Leo asked that Crowe go into the bathroom for his toothbrush and dental powder. When he did, he found that the bristles of the brush were all nearly flat.

After he finished running the nub of the brush over his teeth, Leo smiled. “I have one more favor to ask of you, if I may.”

He asked Crowe to go to his closet and retrieve a suit of clothes. Then he sat on the edge of the bed, slowly working his swollen fingers through the task of buttoning a dress shirt. He asked that Crowe help him with the topmost button. Tucking the shirt into his pants, he then jump-roped a tie over the back of his neck and began the task of tying it. Crowe helped him cinch the knot up snug just under the bump of his Adam's apple.

Standing steadily, he put his arms back and let Crowe slide the sleeves of the threadbare jacket up and over his hands to the shoulders.

"Ah, a valet."

"Yes, my lord," Crowe said, smiling. He walked around to the front of him. "I don't know, Leo, looking like you do, you might find a wife yet."

Leo laughed and asked him to walk near him as he made his way to the bathroom.

"Are you sure?"

He nodded. "I feel twenty years younger," he said, though he gripped Crowe's arm for support.

Standing in front of the mirror, the old man admired himself, smoothing his hand back over his fresh haircut. "Yes, this is how a gentleman should look."

Crowe took him by the elbow and lead him back into the bedroom and then to the bed. Leo pulled up the comforter and then lay on top of it.

"Do you want me to put your clothes away?"

He shook his head. "I'll be fine. I'd like to stay this way for a while." He laughed. "In the space of an hour, you've seen me wear an entry rug and now my best suit."

"I prefer this look," Crowe said as he gathered the toiletries. "I'm going to be back again to check on you tomorrow, okay? Sleep well, Leo."

"I believe I will. And thank you… for everything."

Crowe reached down and squeezed his knobby hand. Leo squeezed back as best he could.

Returning to his apartment, Crowe put everything back into its place. The memory of Leo's grateful face kept a smile on his own. It had turned out to be a good night. He could still feel the wisps of hair between his fingers as though they were still there. Pulling up his blankets, he shut off his bedside lamp and closed his eyes. Tonight he would sleep, he was sure of it.

"You deserve it, you are a cheating whore, Anya!"

"Sam, I will never again feel safe around you. Never again!"

Crowe had forgotten that he'd taken the towel from the vent up to Leo's apartment. By hearing their hateful, subterranean voices, he could feel his exhaustion return, and the idea of retrieving the towel from the hamper overwhelmed him. He turned one ear into the mattress and pressed his pillow over the other, smothering their endless stream of arguing and insults down to a murmur.

CHAPTER 2

His brow damp with sweat, Crowe stood outside the fire door on the landing of the 77th floor. It was the highest he'd ever reached. He'd had the good luck of following closely behind a maintenance worker on the stairs as she swiped her passkey through security gates on each landing. Listening to music from receivers stuffed into each ear, she hadn't heard Crowe behind her, sprinting up the steps and catching each door before it fully closed. For whatever reason, she wasn't using the service elevator, and it was a stroke of luck that set his heart racing as he'd ascended flight after flight.

Early on, ACT had been able to provide him with a small stipend for bribing security guards. It was never enough to get him very far. Then, he discovered that he could talk to the guards and find out what they needed beyond money. It was a weakness in the Board's approach to keeping order in the building. Most of the guards lived on the 21st and 22nd floors in rent-subsidized apartments. Their pay provided for little beyond their basic needs and many of them had families. By spending some of his evenings tutoring the children of security personnel for free, Crowe had been able to move seamlessly between the 30th and 50th floors. It was a way as well to educate young people about the realities of the building they were living in. Many of his sample math problems could be related to calculating the load and juxtaposing it with the building's tensile strength. He couldn't indoctrinate directly, but sometimes, like the week before, a child might ask the right questions.

The thin, bright-eyed seventh-grader had looked up from her homework. "What happens if the live load is bigger than the tent style strength?"

Crowe smiled and shook his head. "Tensile."

"Tensile," she repeated.

He looked behind him and confirmed that the child's mother was still absorbed in a television program. "That's an interesting question."

She looked at him intensely. "What could happen?"

Crowe scratched his head. "I'm not sure. What do you think could happen?"

She looked down at the paper and then up at him again. "What is that again… tensile strength?"

He stroked his chin thoughtfully. "I don't know." He asked her if maybe she wanted to research it.

She skated her small finger over the cracked screen of her digital pad. He let her try, and when she couldn't do it, he spelled the word for her.

"Here it is! It says tensile strength is 'the resistance of a material to breaking under pressure.'"

Crowe pumped his palm softly toward her. "Shh, shh." He looked again toward the mother whose attention pivoted between her own digital pad and the television.

"Could something bad happen to the building?"

He pulled at an earlobe thoughtfully. “I don’t know. Do you think it could?”

Scrunching her nose, she scratched the tip. “It sounds like too much live load isn’t good.”

He looked up at the ceiling and then back at her. “I never thought of that. Sounds like it could be true. Maybe.” Then, before she said more, “We should probably take a look at your history essay now.”

While he corrected her grammar, she had tried several times to bring the conversation back to the building, but he reminded her that she needed to concentrate on the matter at hand. Still, he had stolen glances at her pensive face and could almost hear the wheels turning in her developing brain.

The pristine fire door in front of him opened to his knocking. Standing before him was a bald-headed guard looming some four inches in height above him with broad shoulders. They’d met a week before in the rec room on Crowe’s floor. “If you get up to the 77th,” the guard had said, handing Crowe a digital pad, “we can do this.” Beyond him was a hallway of bright light fixtures, freshly painted walls, wrought-iron benches, and a stretch of shampooed carpet. A Brahms concerto played softly through the hallway’s speakers.

“You made it. Do you have it?” the guard asked.

Crowe reached into his satchel and retrieved the digital pad that he handed to the guard. “It’s in your documents under Vows.”

The guard slid his thick finger over the screen and began reading. His tough face changed, softened. “This is nice. She’ll like this.” He kept reading. “I couldn’t have written anything like this.”

Crowe had to admit to himself that he'd been thinking about his feelings for Dagmar the entire time he was writing the guard's wedding vows. He couldn't imagine sharing any of what he'd written with her. She'd have thrown the pad across the room. He knew too that the words might just be a projection of what he wanted to feel… idealizing something that wasn't ideal.

The guard smiled. "Jesus, she's going to cry."

Crowe opened his satchel and thumbed through his copies of fliers and pamphlets.

The guard studied him. "So, what's to keep me from pushing you back through that door and locking it?"

"A sense of fairness," Crowe said. Then: "Or knowing that there's a remote access virus that can easily corrupt that file."

The guard grabbed him by the shirt collar and pressed him against the wall. He looked back down the empty hallway and then into Crowe's eyes. "You're pretty clever, aren't you?"

He averted his eyes to the floor. A cello flourished in the speakers.

"Okay, I need to make my rounds. If someone has a problem with you, and you mention me, there'll be hell to pay." He pushed past Crowe and ascended the stairs. The door shut behind him.

Crowe quickly discovered a difference between the new floor he was on and others that he had canvassed. Not only were the hallways more opulent, but each door was equipped with a video monitor for the threshold. It was easy enough to step out of the periphery of a peephole, not so a wide-angle lens. Not one of the first twenty doors he tried opened for him or even acknowledged him through the intercom. From many, he could hear people inside moving around or talking, but they only needed one glance at him through the monitor to decide against opening the door.

For each, his only alternative was to slide a pamphlet across their sill. It was purely informational with accurate descriptions of dead load versus live load. Nearly five years ago, the Board had voted to add five new penthouse floors to the building, significantly increasing the dead load. The exoskeleton was constructed at the same time, which as they explained, not only offset the additional weight but even added to the overall structural strength of the building. When writing this part of the pamphlet that detailed the Board's decision, Crowe used, as often as he could, the word, "alleged."

What the pamphlet focused on most was the variable—and therefore more dangerous—live load. His pamphlet gave examples of how live load could be reduced if individuals took responsibility for their effect on it. Not only should new purchases be considered in the face of their effect on load, but the even more socially conscious action would be to jettison any heavier items already included in the household.

Dagmar had argued with him over the use of the word 'jettison' but he liked its allusion to aircraft and boats discarding items to stay in flight or afloat.

The video monitor to the side of the door in front of him flashed with light and a woman's beleaguered face appeared on it.

"Who is it?"

Crowe guessed that the woman was in her late sixties or early seventies. She wore a black dress. In the shallow depth of field of the screen, he could make out the blurry outline of a seven or eight-person sectional sofa. He leaned in closer to the screen.

"My name is Harvey Crowe."

She asked him what he wanted.

"I'd like to talk to you for a moment if I could."

She too leaned in closer, and her face warped into a fishbowl effect. He wondered if his was doing the same and pulled back.

"There's no soliciting on this floor, young man."

"No, no, no… I'm not selling anything. I'm a community activist. I just want to talk to you about the condition of the building on the lower levels."

She said that sounded like a conversation for the Board, not a recent widow.

Crowe swallowed. "I'm sorry for your loss. I didn't know—"

She nodded and muttered as though speaking to herself. "The funeral was three days ago." As though hearing the reality of what she'd just said, she put her hand over her mouth and looked near tears.

He still remembered the early days after his parents' deaths. "It gets quiet fast, doesn't it?"

She seemed to be studying him. Then she nodded. "It does. The phone stops. The visitors stop. People go back to their lives. It's as though I finally have time to be sad, and now I'm drowning in it." She said that her son was staying with her, but that he intended to go back to his unit the next day. "We're only a few floors apart, but once he gets back to his practice, it's like he might as well be on another planet."

Crowe thought of Leo and said to himself that he needed to visit him.

She sighed. "It's as though I feel more alone now than when I first learned that he died."

"I recall that feeling," he said, nodding. "My parents died two years ago."

She tilted her head in the screen. "Both of… but you're so young."

"They didn't die of natural causes." Because she asked, he told her about the snapped gas line, the carbon monoxide that snuck in like an assassin and suffocated them in their sleep.

"They are the reason I became an activist."

She wanted to know more, and he told her about the cracks in the walls and the complicity of the tenants. While he spoke, two different doors opened in the hallway. Two heads, one a man's and one a woman's, looked at him, then at each other, and then closed their doors.

Another classical piece by Mozart was playing out of the speakers.

"But, the Board," she said. "They have weight restrictions for each tenant. And then the exoskeleton."

Always the exoskeleton. People invoked its mention as though it were a benevolent god.

He told her that the weight restrictions weren't enforced. "They're a placebo. They have no way of knowing how much live load is in the building. And any gains made from the exoskeleton were negated when they added more floors." Dagmar always said the members of the Board weren't necessarily evil but were a healthy mix of corruption and naïve optimism, which was just as bad. Somehow money was involved she suspected – kickbacks from the merchandise companies, bribes from contractors, hush money from the most culpable tenants.

The woman sighed, her pale face a portrait of sadness. "I do plan to downsize," she said. She said in the next month she would move to a smaller apartment. "I'll probably get rid of some of the furniture."

"Anything helps," he said, "And, I'm sorry, I know this is a difficult time to be thinking about anything other than your grief."

"Oh," her face changed, showing a sudden recognition. "My husband was a collector... he collected medical books." She touched her fingers along her chapped lips and smiled. "I mean, he was a doctor, so it interested him. But there's a whole room in here just for the books. There has to be over 3,000." She shook her head. "I don't know what I'm going to do with them."

Crowe imagined the books – not one-pound paperbacks, but hard cover medical books with hundreds and hundreds of pages and thick illustration pages. Calculating in his head, he guessed that there could be eight to twelve thousand pounds of load in that room... maybe more.

Synapses fired in his brain. If the Board could fabricate, so could he. And it wasn't so much a fabrication as an epiphany. He was certain Dagmar could gather a few people to help. He cleared his throat. "Ma'am, our group provides a service in these circumstances. We could move the books for you and—"

She smiled. "Forgive the pun, but they have been weighing on my mind. It would be wonderful if—"

"Mom, who are you talking to?"

A man's glowering face leaned into the screen, blocking hers. He studied Crowe for a moment. "Who is that?"

"I'm—"

He turned back towards his mother before Crowe could answer. "Are you talking about Dad's books? Nobody's taking Dad's books. He wanted me to have them."

"Well, David, this young man said— David?!"

His head disappeared. A moment later the door to the apartment opened. The man fuming in front of Crowe couldn't have been much older than him. He wore sweat pants and a t-shirt and everything about his hair said he'd just woken from a long sleep.

"Who the hell are you?"

"David?" his mother's voice called out from the tiny speaker.

He turned to the screen. "Mom, stay out of this. I told you not to talk to anyone. The only people that come around at a time like this are jackals."

She began to cry and then the video screen went gray before fading to black.

David turned back to Crowe. "So, what gives… is there some kind of notification system in the building that lets you know when there's a vulnerable widow?"

"No… I…"

"No… I…" David repeated, mocking the high pitch of Crowe's voice. He pointed toward his mother's apartment door. "That woman just lost her husband of 43 years. Do you have any idea what that book collection is worth?" He held his hand up in Crowe's face. "Don't bother. I'm sure you do."

Down the hall, the door from the stairwell opened, revealing the guard that had let Crowe in. Seeing Crowe being confronted by a tenant, his face blanched.

"Hey," David called, "you want to do your job and get this trespasser out of here? Where the hell have you been, anyway?"

He started to say something about monitoring other floors, but then cut himself off and marched toward Crowe. His neck was enflamed red up to his ears.

Crowe held up his hands at his approach. "I—"

"Shut up, scum bag." In seconds, Crowe's arm was wrenched behind his back and the guard's other arm was around his throat. Wrestling Crowe towards the fire door, the guard called back over his shoulder: "Sorry, Mr. Montgomery."

In reply, David slammed the door to his mother's apartment.

"I can't—"

A hot breath in Crowe's ear hissed. "Can't what? Can't breathe? Good." He slammed Crowe into the fire door, opening it, and then released him on the landing. "I thought you were just handing out fliers!"

He rubbed his aching elbow. "I was. I was just talking to this woman, and then her son went ballistic."

"Yeah, I'll bet." The guard pushed open the gate at the top of the stairs. He shoved Crowe, who grabbed the railing to keep from falling down to the next landing. When he turned to look, the guard was still holding his satchel. He threw it in the air above Crowe where it opened and rained down pamphlets, fliers, and brochures all over him and the stairwell.

The guard pointed a menacing finger at him. "And if you even think about erasing those wedding vows, I will find you and I will hurt you. Bad." He turned, slipped his pass key into the fire door, and marched back onto the floor. The door slammed behind him, its resonance echoing all around Crowe as he stooped to collect his literature.

Descending the stairs in defeat, he heard the straining gears of one of the driverless delivery trucks snaking its way up the freestanding service road that wound along the outside of the building to the Receiving Bay on the 25th floor. The Receiving Bay had a scale, but Dagmar had evidence from a woman that worked in Deliveries that the bulk of cargo was off-loaded before the trucks ever drove onto the scale. Comparing the incoming scale numbers to a live load census that had been taken 15 years ago and then subtracting from that the scale numbers collected from the Outbound and Refuse Bays, the Board reported that there had been no significant change to the live load in all those years. Dagmar doubted the accuracy of the initial census and numbers coming from the Outbound Bay. He heard the muted squeal from the truck's hydraulic brakes—the vehicle itself stopping, he imagined, some ten feet from the scale. He exhaled a despondent breath of air.

Back in his apartment, he sat at his table spinning a forkful of noodles through the vegetable oil in front of him. Across from him, Dagmar perched on the other chair with her legs crossed under her. Her hair was drying from a shower she'd just taken in his bathroom. In front of her sat her own plate of untouched noodles.

"You should eat," Crowe said, taking a bite.

"I'm not hungry."

"Stay on your side of the line, goddamnit, Anya!" The super's voice sounded as though he were shouting into a tin can.

Dagmar looked up, a nick of a smile on her face. "What is that?"

Crowe looked over his shoulder toward the bedroom. "Nothing. An idiot."

She snickered and then turned her attention back to Crowe's latest copy of STORIES.

He stabbed and then twisted his fork into the noodles. "Some board members have to care, I think. They would be willing to listen."

"Name one."

He set down his fork with a wad of pasta wrapped around it. "LaMark for one. I ran into him last night. He was doing some investigating of the lower floors for himself."

She scratched her cheek absently. "I have heard good things. He seems to care. Not about the crucial things, but he cares."

He picked the fork up toward his mouth and then set it down again. He held his arm out in front of him and rotated his wrist, trying to stretch some of the pain from his elbow. "If we could get him to listen, maybe we'd make some inroads."

She turned her attention back to Crowe's newsletter. "I suppose."

"But then," he said, "not very likely when most people think of ACT as a collection of goons and hooligans now. Do you think—"

She looked up. "What is this that you wrote in here about Operation Steel?"

"What?"

She looked down and then read aloud: "'We can be hopeful that the steel pilings will add some needed stability to the building's structure.'" She looked up with a sneer on her face. "What is that? Are you writing propaganda for the Board now?"

"Propagan— are you serious? I could have had my neck broken today falling down a stairwell. And that's kind of thanks to you and the rest of your roughnecks. Are you doubting my—"

She crumpled the newsletter in her fist. "Our direction is changing, Crowe. Complacent sentiments like this can't be seen coming from us."

"Complacent? I'm only reporting the truth of—"

She stood up swiftly. "The truth? 'We can be hopeful'? How in the hell is that the truth? There's nothing to be hopeful about. Every indication points to the inevitability of a complete building collapse in the next six months… a year at most. You're writing Pollyanna daydreams." She dropped the crumpled paper into her noodles, like the specter of a giant meatball. "You need to remember the vigilance you had when you joined. Get your head out of the sand."

She glared at him, and the disgust he saw in her eyes broke his heart.

"I'm sorry."

She walked to the door and opened it. "Don't be sorry. Do something. Your parents died because of the Board's neglect. Don't forget that. Keep your promises." She stormed out, slamming the door behind her.

She was right. Words weren't doing anything. How many copies of STORIES had he distributed? How many leaflets, handouts, tracts, and exhaustive white papers? He'd knocked on hundreds of doors only to be met with indifference, pity, hostility, or silence.

He looked to his left and spotted a new crack splintering across the wall. Had he not seen it before? It seemingly appeared overnight, like a spider spinning up a web in the quiet hours of darkness—some natural, persistent force slowly trapping all of them.

"Keep your promises," he heard again in his mind and then suddenly sprang up from his seat and out the door.

He took the stairs two at a time, and when he finally reached the door, he stuck its key in it.

"Leo?" he called. "I'm here. It's me, Harvey Crowe. I'm sorry if you were expecting me sooner."

A dusty clock on the wall told him it was quarter after nine, and he guessed that the old man had already gone to bed. "Leo?"

Crowe went into the bedroom. Leo lay as he had left him the night before on top of the comforter and still in his suit. His hands were folded on his chest and were cold to the touch.

"No."

He dropped to his knees at the side of the bed. Tears slid down his cheeks as he looked at the unmoving body. He waited in vain for a breath to raise the ribcage.

It was as if the old man had known the night before what was coming for him. Working like a mortician, using Crowe as an unwitting assistant, he'd prepared himself, having felt death's cold shadow pass through his small rooms just moments before the young man's arrival.

CHAPTER 3

The funeral was held the next morning in one of the recreation rooms on the 15th floor. Crowe had done what he could to get the word out the night before after reporting the deceased to the liaison on Leo's floor. The cause of death was ruled to be old age.

Still in his suit, his body was laid out on a dusty pool table that hadn't seen use in years. Crowe had spread out Leo's bed sheet to protect the table's felt. The room brought its own melancholy to the occasion with its threadbare carpeting and paint peeling in sheets from the walls. The overhead fluorescent lights flickered sporadically. He'd asked that something appropriate be played through the room's audio system, but learned that the speakers had been stolen and never replaced.

An odor of cadaverine and putrescine permeated the air but was only strong close to the body. Reluctant to have one at all, especially for someone with no kin or friends, the liaison allowed for a ten-minute ceremony.

"I was his friend," Crowe said.

The liaison, her hair pulled into a tight bun, made a noise in her throat of disapproval. "Fifteen minutes, then," she'd said.

Crowe stood at the off-balance bistro table that substituted for a podium and looked out over the attendees. Dagmar sat with a handful of other comrades from the Anti-Collapse Trust. Their somber expressions struck Crowe as obligatory. A few old people were slumped into chairs as though someone had spilled them there like bags of refuse. Two were asleep. Crowe smiled at four of his older students that he tutored. They waved when he noticed them. He nodded to them in return. In the back of the room, wearing ventilator masks and rubber gloves embossed with the silhouette of skull and crossbones, two members of the maintenance department leaned with crossed arms against the wall waiting to take the body to the incinerator.

Crowe checked the time and then cleared his throat. He told the small gathering that they should probably get started. He remembered his parents' funeral… not much grander than Leo's and almost as rushed.

"I'm not sure where to begin…" he paused noticing movement near the back.

The rec room door opened and Director LaMark entered wearing a dark suit. Like the maintenance men, he stood along the back wall. He wasn't as young as Crowe would have guessed. There were details he'd missed in the poor lighting of the stairwell. The gray along his temples and the crow's feet around his eyes suggested late forties or early fifties. Still, he was a cub compared to some of the old lions that had been on the Board for decades.

"Uh… I'm…" Crowe tried to find his words. He made eye contact with LaMark who smiled solemnly and nodded his encouragement.

He cleared his throat again. "I suppose it's fitting that I should be up here. I likely knew Leo better than any of you, and I only knew him for the space of an hour." He looked around the room. Not even the aide had shown up, even though he had left a message with the medical service the night before. He forgave her, guessing that like many others, she was overworked and underpaid. "I wish I could say something more about him beyond the circumstances of our having met." He told them about the phone call, how he'd found Leo shivering at the threshold. The cleansing. The suit. "In a sense, I was conducting his *tahara*." Crowe looked at his students. "In Jewish communities, members of a group called the *chevra kadisha* prepare the body of the deceased for burial. *Chevra kadisha* translates to sacred society. The ritual preparation of the body is called *tahara*. They have a similar practice of cleansing the dead in Islam. And both religions dress the dead in some kind of white linen after the ritual cleaning."

Dagmar gave him a puzzled look.

One of the maintenance men looked at his watch and then nudged his co-worker. They both pulled their gloves on tighter, letting the cuffs snap against their wrists.

"I suppose," Crowe continued, "I'm rambling because I want to say more, but I don't know what else to say about Leo." He pushed his fingers through his hair. "And, yet, it feels like something should…" His voice trailed off.

The maintenance men pulled themselves from the wall, pulling the straps tighter on their ventilator masks. They started towards the pool table.

"Give the man a minute."

They turned to see that it was LaMark that had addressed them. Looking at each other, they shrugged and went back to their places on the wall.

Crowe started again. "It's just when I think about him, he's like many of us in the building…in life." He thought of the woman on the 77th floor whose husband had died. Even with all her money, she'd felt instantly isolated. "We are largely alone. Everyone is so busy… we just don't have time—" He stopped. "But that's not really what I wanted to say, either. What struck me about Leo was even in what I guess he knew to be his final hours, he wanted a little dignity. He didn't want to feel like a burden or feel forgotten or feel disposable. He wanted to feel human." He looked at LaMark who smiled and nodded. "Whatever our circumstances, whatever our skills, whatever our wealth, we all deserve at least a modicum of dignity." He looked out at the faces that seemed to be paying attention. "And dignity is something we feel in ourselves, but receive from others. In Leo's case, it was the most basic of grooming which I, with a little sacrifice, could help him with." He paused and thought of the old man's smile whilst looking at himself in the bathroom mirror. "I think that could be a way for us to remember and honor Leo. We can offer each other the basic dignity that he craved for himself in the last hours of his life." He looked out over the gathering. "Thank you for coming."

A momentary silence fell over the room.

"Amen!" one of the old women in the front row shouted.

"*Chesed shel emet*," spoke another.

Before Crowe could leave the makeshift podium, his students rushed forward. They told him that he had spoken well.

They said they were sorry for his loss. Soon after, they turned the conversation to why they were there: their grades. They told him about grades on papers, grades on quizzes, and their remarkable grades on exams. When Crowe glanced up, he saw Dagmar studying him with the young people gathered around him. With the quizzical look on her face, he guessed she was forming a judgment about his softness, his meekness... the disparity between what ACT needed and what he had to offer. Or was this his evaluation of himself? He wasn't quite certain what to read into her smile as she watched the children clamoring around him.

At the back of the room, the maintenance men strode forward towards the pool table. They approached with all the emotion of men who had finally been given the green light to drain and disinfect a filthy swimming pool.

"Come on, come on," Crowe said, ushering the children towards the door and away from the act of Leo about to be carried off like an old rug.

Walking behind them with his arms outstretched, Crowe looked over his shoulder toward Leo lying in repose. The maintenance men stood on opposite ends of the pool table. They lifted the corners of the sheet, hoisting Leo's body inside what ended up looking like a stain-covered hammock. They hauled him to the door near the back corner of the room. Struggling with the dead weight, the man in the front shot out a hand, opened the door, and then just as quickly reapplied his double-handed grip. Lurching forward, they faltered a moment. Crowe heard the distinct sound of Leo's head knocking into the door frame. After a moment, the men readjusted their trajectory and disappeared with their cargo through the doorway.

"By George, be careful!" Crowe shouted. He shook his head. For all of his speech-making and his talk of human dignity, those two hadn't heard a word of what he had said.

Looking for him in the hallway, Crowe realized that LaMark too had left. He had hoped to talk to him… to at least thank him for coming. Did he even remember him from the stairwell? What was he even doing at Leo's sad little funeral?

A face emerged through the fog of his musing close to his own.

Dagmar.

"I'll see you tonight," she said.

"Okay," he said, uncertain if they'd made plans or if maybe her shower simply wasn't working again. She'd said her water pressure lately was like that of a prostate patient's stream of piss. He had to admit that she had a special way with words.

Some of the younger children still huddled around Crowe's legs.

Dagmar looked down at them and then at him. "They like you."

He shrugged. "I talk to them. I listen." He rubbed his forehead. "What's tonight, again?"

She shook her head and exhaled. "Council of Lies?"

Like that, he remembered. Tonight was the board meeting.

Dagmar reached out and squeezed his shoulder. "Nice eulogy." Without making further eye contact, she turned and walked away, the memory of her brief touch lingering on his shoulder for the rest of the day.

That evening they gathered in the rec room on Crowe's floor. The recreation in the space amounted to half a dozen folding chairs and a television mounted to the wall, its screen a spider's web of cracks. Nearly a year ago, responding to what they claimed was the tenants' desire for a more inclusive board meeting, the Board switched from public meetings to televised meetings.

At the time, Crowe had to admit that the board room could get very crowded, and sometimes people were turned away. People could still attend in person if they really wanted, but most preferred the comfort of watching from their living rooms, if they watched at all. Dagmar, though, had a sixth sense for seeing through the Board's benevolence. "How gracious," she'd said. "Now they don't have to deal with much in the way of public comment or questions."

Crowe unfolded one of the chairs and set it next to Dagmar's. A couple of the other members of the Anti-Collapse Trust grabbed chairs of their own. They were a ragged-looking group of what looked like gang members and a sprinkling of meek college students.

"They never say hello to me," Crowe said.

Dagmar looked over her shoulder at the others and then back at Crowe. "I'm sure one of them will still ask you to the formal."

He turned toward the screen. "Funny." He could see her smiling in his peripheral vision. "Why do we even watch these things?"

"Good to know the lies we're up against," she said.

The television switched from a test signal image to a broadcast of the dozen board members and the chairman sitting at a half-circle table looking out over a nearly empty room of chairs. The camera would switch to closeups any time someone would talk at any length, and more often than not that someone was Chandler Burke, the Board's chairman. He liked the meetings to go efficiently, but even more, he seemed to relish any reason to move the meeting into a closed session.

Burke had a head of thick gray hair and a chiseled jawline. His build suggested that he'd played indoor football through his teens and maybe even into college. Two years before, after one of the board meetings, a student activist had pulled a butterfly knife on Burke. It was a story almost mythical in its retelling around the building of how the chairman had quickly disarmed the young man. The attempted stabbing led to the student being banished from the building. Given the witnesses, but especially the knife, nobody paid any attention to the young man's pleas of coercion, manipulation, and innocence.

"If I ever had the chance to get close enough, I'd spit right in his goddamn face," Dagmar hissed, staring at Burke on the screen.

Crowe winced at her rage.

With a bang of his gavel, Burke called the group to order. First, they approved the agenda and the minutes from the last meeting. A series of committee-related reports followed. One committee reported that after extensive research they'd determined that beige would be a more psychologically pleasing color for the hallway carpeting over gray. The vote was then motioned, seconded, and approved without discussion for the installation of new carpeting in the hallways to begin.

Burke knocked his gavel and smiled. "Over the months, I made my displeasure with this committee's lack of expediency known. I suppose now, though, the results were worth the meticulous approach. I hereby dissolve the Ad Hoc Carpet Selection Committee."

Crowe thought of the frayed carpeting in the hallways on his floor. They would surely begin the carpet project on the upper floors and work their way down. It might be years before they reached his floor if they ever did. He could imagine what Dagmar was thinking: "Oh good, a smoldering pile of rubble with brand new, psychologically-pleasing beige carpet swirled through it."

The camera remained focused on Burke. He announced that Operation Steel would begin later that week.

"Precautionary operation, my ass," Dagmar hissed. "Desperate operation is more like it."

A few of the other ACT members grumbled their disapproval of Burke with hers.

Burke cleared his throat. "After working with contractors and assessing outcome versus financial outlay, it has been determined that the more prudent choice was to reduce the steel pilings from 20 to 10. Our architects assure us that the resulting structural reinforcement will bear very nearly the same results." He took a moment and looked around the room, smiling. "This is very good news for Operation Living Space." He went on to explain that though the building tenants had done their part over the last decade to keep the population in check, there was still a growing need for more space. A committee had determined that the solution would be to add more floors rather than expand horizontally at the base of the building. "Much of the need for living space is coming from the upper floors according to a recent census. There are tenants with the means to move into luxurious penthouse apartments that will be made available with the addition of three news floors." He explained that, subsequently, a natural "moving up" would follow as space was vacated. "In the end, all floors would be positively impacted by Operation Living Space whereas the previously researched Operation Horizontal Expansion had severe limitations for having an overall building impact."

Most of the board members could be heard applauding off-screen.

Dagmar crossed her arms and sneered at Burke's face on the television. "Operation Steel was never about addressing load issues. Snakes… they're all snakes."

A styrofoam cup sailed over their heads and hit the screen, spraying it with coffee that appeared to drip down over Burke's face. Startled, Crowe looked over his shoulder to where the other ACT members were slapping each other with high fives. Staring at the screen, Dagmar raised her fist in solidarity.

This won't do, Crowe thought.

The camera snapped out to a wider angle showing the entire board.

"We have no old business to address," Burke said, raising his gavel, "and since I'm assuming that there's no new business—"

Near the far end of the table, LaMark raised his hand.

Burke slowly lowered his gavel, staring at LaMark. "Director LaMark?"

"I would like to make a motion to reallocate funding that would have upgraded recreation rooms on the 80th, 81st, and 82nd floors toward an effort instead to ameliorate the lighting issues on the 1st floor up to the 15th floor."

Both Crowe and Dagmar sat forward in their seats.

"Am I having a stroke?" Dagmar asked.

Burke stared at LaMark for a moment with a look of disbelief. "Are you suggesting that the months of work by the Recreational Update Ad Hoc Committee should be forsaken—"

"Point of order," LaMark said. "The chairman is jumping to discussion before we've had a second in favor of the motion."

The camera cropped in close on Burke who, seeming to sense it, allowed his grim expression to rise slightly into a grin. "Indeed. Do I have a second?" His gaze pivoted around the room, daring anyone to speak. "Hearing none—"

"So moved."

The camera snapped out wide again. Director Peoples, a soft-spoken woman from the 50th floor, sat with her hand raised. She was among the two African American members of the board. Crowe was certain it was the first time he'd ever heard her voice, but then she too was a newer member.

Dagmar rubbed her palms together. "What in the hell is going on? Burke looks ready to burst."

"Before we move to the discussion," Burke started, "I propose that we move into a closed session given the sudden nature of the motion."

"Point of order," LaMark said, standing. He waited.

Burke crossed his arms. "The Chair recognizes Director LaMark."

"The Chairman is moving a discussion into a closed session that has nothing to do with circumstances that would warrant a closed session in accordance to our board bylaws."

The Board had a long history of going into closed session, and nobody had ever questioned Burke's or any chairman's legitimacy to make such a move. Crowe's heart raced. He rubbed his palms dry on his thighs. Go, LaMark! he thought.

Burke explained that the Chairman reserved the right to move the Board into a closed session at his discretion. "You're a relatively new member, Mr. LaMark, so may be unfamiliar with past protocol. In this instance—"

LaMark interrupted. "Then I would like to make a motion that the full board vote as to whether or not—"

"No need," Burke said, squeezing the handle of his gavel. "The point is well taken. You may be seated." He looked around the room and then back to LaMark. "Discussion?"

LaMark adjusted himself in his seat. He opened a file folder in front of him. "Upon casual observation and then with further investigation, I have determined that nearly 60% of the sconces on the first 15 floors are burned out. Of the remaining working lights, another 50% are either flickering or dim. Additionally, and I will admit my observations are anecdotal on this front, the upper floor rec rooms scheduled to be remodeled are virtually unused. Furthermore, their condition does not, in my opinion, warrant a remodel, and they are in much better condition and more recreational than the rec rooms on all the lower floors."

Crowe looked around the rec space they were sitting in. A few months ago, it did contain a pool table, but no sticks and only six balls. The Anti-Collapse Trust had taken it upon themselves to move the table to the Refuse Ramp. Nobody ever complained, and the maintenance department made no effort to return it to its place – a rare load-related victory to the tune of 700 pounds.

LaMark passed out photographs. "These are pictures of the hallways in question, highlighting some of the worst areas. In some instances, you will see nothing in the photograph because the picture was so underexposed by the lack of light." He held up the picture, not for the other members to see, but for the broadcast crew to zoom in on. They didn't, but even from a distance, anyone could see that the picture was nearly black.

Dagmar stood and began pacing the room behind Crowe. "This guy's a snow job," she said, "A plant. He's on the Board to provide the veneer of compassion. Something worse is coming, believe me."

"I think he's the real deal," Crowe countered. "Why else would Burke try for a closed session?"

"We'll see."

Many of the board members passed the pictures on dismissively, as though they'd been handed a plate of earwax cookies to enjoy. A few did examine the images and shook their heads or pursed their lips incredulously.

"Those pictures alone reveal that this has gone from what could have been described as an annoying situation to a dangerous one," LaMark said. "Liability for any accidents or crimes that happen as a result of that darkness will certainly be placed at the Board's feet."

Burke waited a moment. "Mr. LaMark, that's a great deal of research and initiative given your thus far short tenure on the Board. Perhaps you should have chaired the Carpet Replacement Ad Hoc Committee." He chuckled hollowly and then looked around the table. "Other discussion?"

No argument could be made to the necessity of refurbishing the rec rooms in question, but other motions were made. One called for replacing half of the lighting now and the other half to be determined for a later date. It was voted down. Another amendment suggested that an ad hoc committee be formed to determine another fiscal avenue for paying for the lights. That too was voted down. A third motion called for tabling the original motion given the complexities and ambiguities of the situation. The motion to table received a second.

"Point of order." It was Director Peoples again. She pushed aside the hair dangling across her glasses. "Table it? Chairman Burke, there is no other urgent or pressing business to attend to. We have nearly an hour of meeting time remaining with which I am certain we can untangle the 'complexities and ambiguities' of this simple situation."

Dagmar stopped her pacing and turned toward the screen. "I like her. Feisty."

Crowe nodded. "Me too."

"Well taken," Burke offered through clenched teeth.

LaMark's hand shot up.

"Go ahead."

"Chairman Burke and members of the Board, I offer this as a means to hopefully end the discussion and move to a vote. We are not discussing what kind of music should be pumped into the elevators or the color of the new wallpaper. We are talking about tenants leaving their apartments and not being able to see because it's so dark. That's inhumane, and we are in dereliction of our duties as board members if we allow it to continue. We have funding available for an improvement that doesn't need to happen, and we have a dire situation that needs immediate rectification." Suddenly, he stood up.

Burke banged his gavel. "The gentleman—"

"Ladies and gentlemen of the Board," LaMark continued over the rapping gavel, "this body seldom truly considers the needs of anyone below the 25th floor. It's utterly shameful." He paused a moment and then continued. "Because whatever our circumstances, whatever our skills, whatever our wealth, we all deserve at least a modicum of dignity. Having lit hallways is a basic tenant-right. It's something that this body of co-op representatives can give." He took his seat again to the soundtrack of Burke's hammering gavel and a scattering of applause.

Dagmar sat down next to Crowe. "He just plagiarized you."

"No," Crowe said, shaking his head. "He was inspired. That's something." His heart beat in his chest, matching the intensity of Burke's gaveling. Maybe Leo hadn't died in vain. Maybe in his prophetic way, the old man had willed it.

CHAPTER 4

Crowe pulled his satchel from the hook near his door and slung it over his shoulder. The flaky residue of the powered eggs he'd eaten for breakfast lingered in his mouth. Checking the time, he jogged back to his bathroom. Mrs. Montgomery was going to meet him in ten minutes at the elevator on the 25th floor. He dipped his toothbrush into the minty powder in the cup on his sink and brushed his teeth.

"You sabotaged all of the outlets on my side, Sam! That's not fair!"

"Oh, shut up," Crowe said to the echoing voice of the super's wife in the vents. He rinsed his teeth with the last swallow from a can of Just Like Water. No matter how many times he tried to wash it away, the gritty residue of the tooth powder clung to his teeth, the JLW sliding right over it.

Checking his watch again, he ran to his door and exited into the bright light of the hallway. Nearly 80% of the sconces had new bulbs. In honor of LaMark, some on the lower floors had taken to calling them La-Lights. When his motion had finally come to a vote, the Board had approved it by a 60% majority. LaMark had orchestrated everything so perfectly by keeping the meeting televised. Had they gone to a closed session, the motion surely would have failed. And then there was Director Peoples. Maybe, Crowe thought, if they weren't repulsed by Dagmar's militancy, there would be a way to make LaMark and Peoples their allies… or at least sympathetic ears.

Still, Crowe wasn't certain if the lights were a gift or a burden, throwing the actual condition of the hallway into stark relief as they did. The carpeting, under the bright glare of the light, was more than just frayed. It was a palpable history of the years of dirty shoes that had passed over it without it ever having once been vacuumed. It was a mosaic of grime, dirt, spit, blood, and dust. The walls were their own museum of graffiti – some of it directed at the Board, some at the rich, some just anger made most plain in the form of profanity.

Mrs. Montgomery had surprised him with her foul language when she'd called his telephone just twenty minutes before.

"Is this Harvey Crowe?" she'd asked.

Hesitantly, he'd answered yes. Just the other day, a delivery man had asked him the same question. When Crowe confirmed his identity, he was shoved against the wall. For better or worse, he was becoming known.

"I would like you to come to my apartment." The female voice spoke with a privilege that suggested what she'd said was not a request, but a statement of her wishes that he would certainly fulfill.

"May I ask who this is?"

"It's Mrs. Montgomery."

The name was only vaguely familiar to him. "Mrs--?"

"We spoke just the other day." She paused. "My husband had passed... with the collection of medical books."

He stood up from his kitchen table. The hydrated powdered eggs on his plate were starting to flake apart. "I can meet you."

"Good. I think I'm ready to do something about all of this... shit." She said the word as though it had never been in her mouth before.

Before she could hang up, he explained that it wasn't a matter of him just taking an elevator up to her floor. For one, besides a restricted service elevator, there was no lift for the first twenty-five floors. Five years before, in its initial response to the building's "alleged" structural issues, the Board voted to fill with concrete the first 25 floors of the elevator shaft. Called Operation Core Reinforcement it was implemented under the theory that the procedure, once the concrete cured, would lock parts of the building into place. However, once the operation had been completed, no follow-up structural analysis had been done to determine if it had improved anything. The Board of course spoke in one voice that everything was much improved because of it.

"It did one thing," Dagmar had said when the subject came up between her and Crowe. "It made it so bottom dwellers from the lower floors have no access to the upper floors." She speculated that had been the Board's plan all along and that they'd capitalized on the "hysteria" surrounding load to push their elevator-restricting agenda through. It wasn't long after, that plans for the exoskeleton were discussed.

"I can meet you on the 25th floor then," she'd said, "and we'll ride up together."

He grimaced. "You will have to open the fire door for me. But I'll be waiting right there on the landing. I promise."

She huffed. "This place acts as a prison sometimes but, yes, I will meet you there."

Reaching the stairwell, he checked the time and then started sprinting up the stairs. What if he missed her? She had sounded like maybe she was ready to offload the book collection after all. Maybe her son had decided he didn't have the room for them. Like the hallway, the stairwell too was well-lit, newly revealing its ugliness. The sentiments of the hallway graffiti down below were echoed here as well. Butts and split capsules of stimulant and depressant inhalants littered the steps.

He ascended, hindered only a few times by a security gate still in its place, like a phantom unwilling to leave the place where it died. The locking mechanisms had long since been stripped out and the gates pushed open easily on their rusted hinges. The rest of the landings showed only the holes where the hardware to hold a security gate had been. Crowe ran past all of it until he finally reached the 25th floor. Dripping sweat, he pounded on the fire door.

A security guard opened it. "What?"

Crowe stood, catching his breath, panting. He looked a sight with a mop of sweaty hair hanging into his eyes and his disheveled clothes.

The guard set his hand on Crowe's chest and pushed him back. "Beat it."

"No, I—"

“Let him through. He’s with me,” Mrs. Montgomery said as she strode down the hallway behind the guard.

The guard turned and looked at her. “Are you sure?”

“Quite.” Everything about her groomed appearance and handsome clothes said he’d better listen.

The guard stepped aside and let Crowe pass. Crowe combed his fingers through his wet hair.

“Sorry,” he said, “I just… ran up… 15 flights.”

She told him there was no need to apologize. They walked down the hallway together, neither speaking another word. Walking a few feet behind her, Crowe worked to catch his breath.

The elevator attendant let Mrs. Montgomery in and then blocked out Crowe with his arm. “The elevator is for specific tenants only.”

Mrs. Montgomery rolled her eyes. “Oh for God’s sake, he’s with me.”

The attendant looked at her, assessed her seriousness, and then lowered his arm. Crowe stepped on and stood at Mrs. Montgomery’s side at the back of the elevator. He reached out and steadied himself with his hand against the wall when the elevator wiggled a moment and then started to rise.

“Are you okay?”

He nodded. “I just haven’t been on one in a long time.”

She patted his arm. “Sometimes I think about the cables,” she said and shuddered dramatically for effect.

He then thought about the cables too. He imagined the snap, the rocketing descent, the shattering crash. His shuddering was all too real.

When they arrived at her door, she passed her palm over a metal plate under her video monitor. The door unlocked. He thought of the key in his pocket. The brass teeth were so worn down that it often took him several attempts to activate the tumblers in the deadbolt to get his apartment door to unlock.

Following her, Crowe stepped over the threshold and into her foyer.

She looked at him reaching toward his heel. "No, you don't have to take your shoes off," she said.

He then followed her into the living room where he found hardwood floors, two slipper chairs, and a small coffee table. Otherwise, the room was nearly bare. "Are you moving?"

"No." She explained that she wasn't able to find an upper-floor apartment any smaller than hers. "Bigger? Yes. There's always the option to upgrade. I would have to move down to the 49th floor to get anything smaller and… well, I prefer my neighbors up here."

He smiled and nodded.

"I don't mean… it's just they are the people I'm used to. I need the routine and familiarity right now. It's difficult without Paul."

"That makes sense."

She stood for a minute, her face lost in melancholy thought. Then she threw her hands up into the air. "I'm being a terrible host. Would you like something to drink after all of those steps?"

He used his fingers to tame his sweaty hair. "Maybe just some water?"

She disappeared into her kitchen and then returned with a glass of crystalline beverage. Light from the apartment's sunshine-simulating windows refracted through the water and cast a small rainbow of colors on the floor.

Crowe picked up the glass and turned it in front of his face. "It's so clear. Is this Just Like Water?" Even the smell from it was something pristine... primordial. Like this was the scent that followed when "let there be water" was spoken.

Mrs. Montgomery lowered herself into the opposite chair. "No. I wouldn't even wash my dishes with Just Like Water." She smiled sadly. "My guess is the water in your apartment doesn't look like that?"

He shook his head and then took a drink. His first sip turned into guzzling. His mind went to Leo and what it would have been like for him to have such a basic but intoxicating experience on the night of his death. He set the emptied glass on the table. "My God." He shook his head. "No, the water is not like that in my apartment."

"More?"

Crowe politely declined. "Maybe later."

She picked up the glass and took it to the kitchen. When she returned she was holding a piece of paper. "Then I suppose you didn't get this memo from the co-op board."

Crowe stifled a smirk every time he heard the phrase. Dagmar had insisted on not referring to the building as a co-op. "You like words, Crowe. What is co-op short for?" she'd asked.

"Cooperative."

Sneering, she nodded. "Right. But, there's nothing cooperative about what happens in this place. If anything, we've been co-opted into a system that considers very little of our existence. It's a co-opt board."

He took the paper from Mrs. Montgomery's hand and read about the success of Operation Cistern, which detailed the Board's decision to install a new reservoir that would supply the freshest and safest water possible to the tenants. He could almost feel the blood drain from his face. "No, I did not get this memo." More handiwork from the Board's closed session meetings.

"I didn't think so." She gingerly took the paper from his grip, folded it, and returned it to the kitchen.

When she came back again, she held a fistful of papers. Crowe recognized them immediately as his literature that he distributed from his satchel. "I've been doing some reading myself," she said. She explained that after he'd been ejected from the hallway, she'd gone after him. She didn't find him, but she'd found some of his papers in the stairwell. "I'm sorry about David," she said, collapsing into her seat. "I'm sorry about so much."

Her blue eyes looked different to him from the eyes he'd engaged in the video monitor. Something there now… some shimmering of new understanding.

"Is all of this true?" she asked, holding the papers out toward him. "Never mind, I know it is."

He sat watching her.

She worried the fingers of her hands over each other. "That's why it looks like I'm moving… why the place is so cleared out. I read this, and I read it again. I couldn't stop reading. I didn't want to believe it, but I could feel how it was true. Whatever I wanted to wish away or pretend was hyperbole… I couldn't. In the silence of my grief, without the constants of Paul and our social life, I had time to sit with the reality of this. Even though

David fought me on it, and now is hardly speaking to me, I did away with all unnecessary furniture. Even some of those medical books, that I've been secretly taking to the Refuse Ramp, but it's not enough. It's not." She shook her head and stared at the floor. Then she looked up at him again. "I want to do more."

Crowe smiled. "And I want you to. What that would be off the top of my head I'm not—"

"I'm going to run for the Board." She looked at him and nodded. "Kenneth Fairsmith's seat is up for reelection."

Director Fairsmith had been on the Board for over two decades. Crowe knew him as someone who never offered an idea, hardly said a word, but always voted in a way that supported Chairman Burke. The only time Fairsmith did speak was to second any motion from Burke to move the meeting into a closed session. "That would be a tough seat to get," Crowe said, shaking his head.

She smiled. "Maybe. Maybe not. He has always run uncontested. I have many friends in this building. I have the advantage of the sympathy votes that would go towards a recent widow. I'm okay with exploiting that. My platform would be upper floors friendly, even if my eventual vote and voice would be otherwise. It's a two-year term. I feel I could do a great deal of good in two years, especially with directors like LaMark and Peoples as allies."

"You watched the board meeting?"

"I did, and it was wonderful." She pinned her fidgeting hands between her thighs. "I tried to imagine Paul watching that same meeting. He likely would have disagreed with everything LaMark was saying… maybe would have barked at the screen as was his habit." Her lips buckled in against her teeth as though she might weep. She took a long breath and then exhaled. "My husband wasn't a bad man... he really wasn't. He was like anyone with wealth, whether hard-earned or inherited. He could rationalize any excess, turn any talk of charity into a treatise on free handouts for sloths, and diminish any talk of an existential threat. My own thinking wasn't far from his until recently... until I was alone here and the whole life we had worked for was upended."

Crowe scratched his cheek thoughtfully. "There are quite a few directors just like Fairsmith on the Board."

"Well, there would be one less." She smiled sympathetically. "I know it sounds pie in the sky or a little farfetched, but let's say I've had a revelation. I can't pretend nothing is happening when something is happening."

"No, of course not," Crowe said, "nobody should." He looked at the papers in her hands and smiled.

Mrs. Montgomery followed his gaze. She set the papers on the coffee table and then pointed at them. "These made a difference. You should keep doing what you're doing."

He told her he intended to. "What about your son? Does he know of your intention to run for the Board?"

She nodded. "He supports it... thinks I should be doing something other than sitting in the apartment by myself. He doesn't know where my head is on all of this, so I'm sure he'll campaign for me." She said she'd only spoken to him by telephone. "He's still upset about my downsizing, but I can tell him I just needed a change. I'll tell him I'm looking to get all new furniture... that I needed to clear some of the memories out of this place. He'll think that's a good idea too."

Crowe looked at the floor, at his ragged shoes, and then up at her again. "Why did you want to tell me this?"

She said she needed someone who would understand what she was feeling. "Plus, you can communicate with people on the lower floors about my position. To what extent the Board even counts the votes from the lower floors, I'm not certain." She touched her fingertips over her lips for a moment. "I know people from the lower floors have run for board positions. I also know that nobody below the 50th floor has ever been elected. I don't think that's just by chance."

Crowe nodded. "That's true."

She brushed her palms down the thighs of her skirt. Then, standing, she clapped her hands together. "Well, it's time for me to start canvassing." She bent over, collected the papers, and handed them to him. "It won't do for me to have this in my apartment. And, you'll have to forgive me, but I won't be able to have any more contact with you. No good for anyone to guess where my sympathies lie." She smiled. "You are known, you know? You even have a nickname."

He raised his eyebrows.

"Chicken Little."

He chuckled and shook his head. "Perfect."

She put out her hand for him to shake. The hand he took was soft-skinned and seemingly frail, but her grip was strong. "Maybe closer to the boy who cried wolf, I'd say, but in this instance, the wolf is there, but the villagers, so wanting the boy to be a liar, refuse to see it." She looked him in the eyes, something glinting in the azure hue of her own. "I see the wolf now. I understand the danger."

He swallowed. "Thank you."

Going to the door, she opened it, checked that the hallway was clear, and then had him step out with his fistful of papers. "I'm with you even if it seems at times that I'm not. You'll have to trust that," she said, closing the door swiftly behind him.

Crowe leaned against the wall in the hallway catching his staggering breaths, believing and not believing at the same time. First LaMark and Peoples, and now Montgomery. It could happen, he thought. It was getting close to a coalition. It struck him as fitting that Beethoven's "Wellington's Victory" was playing through the hallway's speakers. He stuffed the papers she'd returned to him into his satchel.

Down the hall, a chime sounded and then a freight elevator opened and two burly men, their uniforms marking them as members of the building's Delivery Guild, wrestled a huge rubberized mattress from the lift.

Right across from the elevator, an apartment door opened, and a man likely in his thirties stepped out wearing a polo shirt and jeans, his outfit casual given the time of day.

"This is the last of it," one of the men said.

Still reeling from the sight of a waterbed being delivered, Crowe's mind said the word: Sunday. "It's Sunday," he muttered, surprised by how often he didn't know what day of the week it was.

Keep holy on the Sabbath, he thought. And at one time keeping holy had meant more than attending service. It meant no work, relaxation, reflection, time with family…

No work, and yet here these two hulking men with sweaty brows wrestled with the ductile material that seemed itself not to want to be delivered, the way it slouched in their grips and leaned away from their task.

"It is the Lord's day," he remembered a pastor from his youth expressing to the down at the heel, ragtag congregation. "Your only labor should be the gentle labor of reflecting on the teachings of the Lord. Love each other as you love yourself… his greatest teaching, a way indeed for us to have the Heaven on Earth of which he spoke." He'd lifted his hands and bowed his head. "Just love each other."

In the last decade, the spiritual service rooms on the lower floors had emptied. The pastors, rabbis, and imams had given up their calling when the people no longer showed up. They had continued to congregate for a time, but they wanted what the holy people could not provide – alms, assistance with bills, new clothing. But by what means could these be provided when the collection plates were handed out among those who would most need their contents? It wasn't enough to be preached to Sunday after Sunday that their reward would be found in the afterlife. He remembered, just before the churches of the lower floors shuttered, seeing graffiti spray-painted in the hallways: "You Can't Eat Love!" He remembered even as a teen thinking, "It's not about the love being its own sustenance, it's about the sustenance that would arrive on the wings of love." Then he shook his head, understanding why he'd likely had such a difficult time with his peers when he was younger.

Only weeks ago, Crowe had stood outside a service room on the 66th floor. The pastor's words were off, askew, twisted, and tweaked to his congregation's desires. "The Lord," he said, "blesses those deserving of blessings. Think of your possessions, your luxuries. Are you blessed in belongings?"

The congregation nodded. "Amen!"

"And so that is your Lord saying, 'These are my people with whom I am most pleased.' Your bounty is a reflection of the Lord's pleasure with the way that you are living. It is an affirmation that you are to continue gathering onto you that which your blessedness deserves."

It had sounded more like a commercial than a service.

The delivery men heaved the mattress across the hallway where it disappeared through the threshold of the young man's apartment.

"Watch out for the statue in the living room!"

Crowe quickly shuffled through the papers in his hand. Yes! he thought. He double-checked the title of the pamphlet: Waterbeds and Load: What You Need to Know.

"Sir?" he asked, slowly approaching the man. "May I speak with you?"

The man turned his attention away from the inside of his apartment. His scowl spoke volumes. "I'm not interested in whatever you're selling. You're not even supposed to be up here."

"I'm not selling anyth… I just wanted to ask you about that purchase. That's a very big bed. Do you live alone?"

The man looked him up and down, nostril sneering. "You turning tricks or something? What the hell do you care about my big bed?"

Crowe shook his head vehemently. He felt a cool sweat on his wrists and forehead. "No, I'm with…" He stopped himself. Telling anyone he was with ACT had become the equivalent of stating that he was with the Homicide Encouragement

League. “I’m just a concerned tenant.” He handed the man the pamphlet.

The man glanced at the title. “Oh hell, get this out of my face.”

“Sir, please, when that mattress is filled with water, it will add nearly a ton of load. I just want you to consider…”

The man turned away and looked into his apartment. “All set?”

The delivery men emerged into the hallway. One wore a thick salt and pepper beard and carried a clipboard. He handed it to the man who in turn handed him the waterbed pamphlet.

The bearded man looked at the pamphlet and then at Crowe. “Hey, it’s Chicken Little.” He turned back to the tenant. “Is he bothering you?”

The young man looked up from finishing his signature on the proof of delivery. “Hmm?” he grunted, looking at Crowe as though he were a housefly. “No. But I would like to know where in hell the security guard is… you guys have any information when it comes to that?”

They both shook their heads. The other delivery man spoke. “These bottom dwellers are like gnats, though. You chase one off and three more come crawling out.”

“We all live in this building,” Crowe said weakly, uncertain of what he was even saying.

The man handed the clipboard back.

The delivery man checked the signature and then looked up. “We got the water started. Should be filled in about an hour and a half.”

The man thanked them curtly and then retreated into his apartment.

The delivery men turned their attention on Crowe. "What are you doing up here, Chicken Little?"

A staccato breath caught in Crowe's throat. "That's… that's not my name."

Grabbing Crowe's shirt front, the bearded man pressed him against the wall. His hot, sour breath was like an assault. "I asked you a question." He paused a moment and then smiled. "You're shaking. Guess you're not so tough when there aren't five of you, huh?" He waited. "I'm going to ask you again, what the hell are you doing up here?"

"I'm… I was a guest…" He caught himself. So stupid, he thought, almost giving Mrs. Montgomery away. "I tutor—"

Three apartments down, a door opened and a couple stepped out into the hallway. The delivery man let go of Crowe's shirt. Pressing the landing operating panel, the couple stood in front of the guest elevator but glanced now and again toward the trio as they waited.

"Let's get going."

The man with the beard tore the waterbed pamphlet into quarters and handed it back to Crowe. "There you go."

One of the men pressed the button and the freight elevator opened. As the doors closed, the bearded man smiled menacingly at Crowe and ran a finger across his throat.

Crowe's pulse beat in his ears. Down the hall, a bell chimed, and the couple entered the guest elevator. After a moment, he found that he could move again. He crouched down, collected the shredded pieces of the pamphlet, and then stuffed them under the young man's door.

Walking to the fire door, he pushed it open and began his descent, his hand trembling on the railing for seven or eight floors.

That evening Crowe stood at his stove, the one burner occupied with rehydrating and heating a package of broccoli, when someone knocked on his door. If it was Dagmar, she was early, but then why wouldn't she be? He'd told her he had exciting news regarding the cause. He hoped he could make it plain to her that Mrs. Montgomery's candidacy for the Board could change the direction of their efforts. That they needed, more than ever, to be cautious in their approach. No more confronting tenants physically or aggressively. No more stealing marble benches from upper floor hallways and bringing them to the Refuse Ramp. Sure, the benches were never used, but 90% of the time they were returned to their place by building maintenance. Dagmar's efforts seemed only to bring contempt for the cause, both from tenants and from the workers. Caution and discipline were to be the key words. He wondered too, in the splendor of recent developments, if it might be the time to tell her his feelings for her.

He spoke as he opened the door. "I had a feeling you might come—" Standing at his threshold were three large men. Crowe stood frozen, one hand on the door and the other hanging limply at his side.

"Hey, Chicken Licken."

Chicken Lick—?

The first fist that landed in his stomach doubled him over. He fell back into his apartment, both arms gripped over his abdomen. Vaguely, through the convulsing pain, he heard the men enter and close the door behind them. Then, a pair of hands like vice grips picked him up and slammed him into the chair at the kitchen table. His head bounced off the wall and his vision blurred. As he stared at his feet, his eyesight came slowly into focus revealing the three pairs of black boots standing semicircle around his loafers.

Slowly, he looked up into the faces that appeared as though they had been taken from a Roman frieze depicting angry gladiators.

"I don't—"

A swift back hand sent his head careening to the side. The taste of blood seeped into his mouth. His sight went black for a moment and then returned.

"For chrissake, don't knock him out."

Crowe's head lolled on his neck. He felt blind drunk. The tingling in his mouth overwhelmed him and he wretched a mixture of blood and bile on the floor.

"Right on my goddamn boot too!"

After a hazy moment, calloused fingertips reached under his chin and lifted his gaze to meet theirs. Their six steely eyes, fists clenched at their sides, and veins snaking up their necks and pulsating along their course.

"You've caused enough trouble," said the man holding his chin. He withdrew his fingers.

Crowe struggled to keep his eyes fixed on theirs, fearing that if he failed, they'd strike him again. Blood dribbled over his lip onto his chin. His stomach felt like giant hands had grabbed him by the ribs and legs and wrung out his abdomen like a wet rag. On the stove, the pot boiled over, the water hissing as it hit the burner.

One of the men moved away, and when he returned, he was holding Crowe's satchel. It looked stuffed full, and he guessed it was every flier and pamphlet in the place… and maybe whatever else he wanted to take. Not that I have anything else, he thought.

The man held the satchel out towards Crowe's face. "You're costing people their paychecks with this crap."

"It's not crap."

His words were answered with another backhand, sending his head reeling in the other direction and leaving his ears ringing. Shut up, he thought. He felt another swell of blood fill his mouth. He spat.

"Consider this your only warning. You go to the upper floors again spreading your lies, we're coming back. Except we'll be angry when we do." He smiled. "Right now, this is us being polite." He grabbed a handful of Crowe's hair and with a swift, piston motion bounced his head off of the tabletop.

Everything went black again. His ears filled with the high pitch of a thousand hearing tests. Slowly, the black became gray. The gray then became the world of his apartment again out of focus. He focused on the three men standing in front of him, the water hitting the stove hissing a soundtrack for the contempt in their faces.

"Stand him up."

Two of the men took his arms and hoisted him to his feet. They held him up, as though they were his friends, worrying whether or not he could stagger home from a drunken revelry that they had all been to together. A swirl of nausea crawled between his skull and the skin of his scalp. The inside of his cheeks tingled. He teetered back and forth on his unsteady legs.

"You're done with this shit," the man with the satchel said, holding the bag out for emphasis.

They turned for the door and opened it. As though drawn on invisible strings that attached his face to their movement, Crowe turned his head to watch them leave as they drifted in and out of focus.

Shut up, he thought. Just let them leave. Let them. They're almost gone. But his mouth and his larynx conspired against the pleading. "This building is going to collapse," he said. "I'm not going to let that happen."

The last man in the doorway turned to look at Crowe, marched across the kitchen, and laid him out with a sweeping haymaker.

CHAPTER 5

"They're scared."

Her voice came into his indecipherable dreams and woke him into the semi-darkness of his bedroom. Crowe blinked his eyes open. Dagmar's outline was sitting on a chair next to his bed. He knew her not only by the spikey-haired silhouette but by her pungent, sweaty odor, which was both body and somehow vaguely antiseptic as if she'd slept in a puddle of anti-freeze. A haunting of the pain was still there, he could feel its looming presence, waiting for him to wake like an estranged, bitter relative attending his bedside with Dagmar. He tried not to move.

As thunder follows lighting, a slight delay had kept the pain from fully hitting him. Then it came. His face ached like it was being squeezed in a vice. He reached up and tenderly touched a knot the size of an egg from where his head had been treated like a racquetball against the table. His abdomen roiled like it had been hollowed and replaced with torment, like a diseased rodent making a nest of his intestines. Dagmar was still talking, but he zoned in and out of her optimistic rant.

"Something is happening," she said. "To feel like you're that much of a threat… to attack you like that? They are scared. Our message must be reaching some important people."

"You're stealing food that I hid away for me, Sam!"

"Liar! I wouldn't want whatever it was that made you so fat."

"I could kill you in your sleep, Sam! I could!"

"You could never waddle yourself across the apartment. You'd have a heart attack in the living room!"

Dagmar stood up like a shadow moving across the room.

Crowe watched her. "What are you—"

She stomped her boot against the vent and then bent her mouth close to it. "Shut up, you goddamn morons!"

He tried to sit up, but the searing in his gut sent his head back to the pillow. "Dagmar, don't." Even as he protested, he noticed that her approach had worked. The super and his wife had stopped quarreling. The vent went back to breathing its recycled air into the room.

"Don't? What are you talking about? That's the only thing assholes like that understand. Meet venom with venom." She walked back to the chair, sat, and then reached her hand toward the darkness of the floor. When she came back up, she offered a fistful of cold out to him. "Frozen peas," she said.

He took the makeshift ice pack and pressed it to his face. "Thank you."

They sat in silence for a moment. The cold stung his skin at first but then soon numbed the sharp edges of the pain.

"You're too timid, Crowe."

A different pain struck him then in his chest. It was as though she could instinctively expose his own hidden, shameful thoughts of himself. "What? What are you saying?"

"Did you even fight back?"

He fought the urge to sit up. "There were three of them."

"That's not what I asked."

Seeing himself through her eyes, shame washed through him like a virus, chilling him with what seemed like a sudden fever. "No. I didn't know what was happening. It happened fast. I felt like I was watching it happen."

"Like you were frozen."

He thought about it. "I defended myself. I got the last word in." Even as he spoke, he knew it was weak.

Dagmar laughed. "Words, Crowe. Is that all you have?" She stood up and paced the room, darkness of a human form stalking the duskness of the room. "Classic fight or flight. You didn't run… how could you? So, you shut down and just took it."

He wanted her to leave. Everything that was washing back in his mind was too much. His childhood of being the only kid in classes who seemed to take the subjects seriously. The bullying. The fights where he did nothing but take the blows, but later comforted himself under the blankets of his bed that it was the superior way. Pacifism… a word not available to him at the time, but how he later used it to rationalize and even praise the docile behavior of his younger self. Even his father, a timid man himself, crouching, dabbing the sting of mercurochrome to a cut under Crowe's eye had said: "Son, you can fight back. I know I've said violence isn't the way, but in some cases, it's needed. They won't stop until you do."

He never did. And they never stopped.

But then they eventually did stop. In the later grades, he figured out his own way. Negotiation. He would help his bullies in their classes. What they'd heard at first was that he'd do their homework for them. What he had explained in turn was that was no good. There were tests. There were quizzes. They needed to know the material themselves to pass. Even though their disdain for education hadn't changed from their elementary years, they realized as they aged that they needed to do at least something. That they needed to pass. And so they 'allowed' Crowe to tutor them. He could still recall one of his worst tormentors softly slugging him in the shoulder after earning a C+ on a math exam. "You're alright, Harvey," he'd said.

The recollection of that moment had always been fond for him. Still, lying in his bed, his face a batik of bruises, he wondered if tutoring them had just been another form of cowardice… prostituting his brain to protect his body.

Then, the memory of events that had happened just an hour before came to him. When the last man rushed him from the doorway to knock him out cold… had he stuck out his chin to take it, as though he deserved it? Had he turned the other cheek only to have it nearly caved in?

"Maybe you're right," he said, almost whispered. The idea of expressing to her his feelings about them—his feelings for her—felt ridiculous. If she didn't loathe him, she certainly at best pitied him.

She sat down again. "What did you say?"

He didn't repeat himself. It was enough to admit to himself the truth of her perception. He took the frozen peas from his face and let them slump to the floor. "Do you even know why I wanted to talk to you tonight?" he asked. "I mean, the exciting news I mentioned on the phone didn't have anything to do with me being assaulted." It hurt for him to talk, but he couldn't let her leave, couldn't end on a note of defeat.

The silhouette in front of him crossed her arms. "So what was it?"

The good news of it came to him again. It eased the pain, and he spoke at length about Mrs. Montgomery. The feelings of hope he'd felt when he'd left her apartment surged through him. Gaining allies from the upper floors was the only way they were going to tackle the problem of the building's future.

"I don't trust it," Dagmar said after he'd finished. Her voice, her words, came into the room like a soaked blanket over the embers of his optimism.

"Don't trust it? What are you talking about?"

She stood again and prowled the room, a phantom of despair in the low light. "What if it's a ruse? What if she's only doing it to get votes from the lower floors?"

He shook his head. "That doesn't make sense." He crossed his arms. "And I more than half-suspect she's right that the lower floor votes aren't even counted."

Dagmar made a noise in her throat that expressed her doubt.

"Seriously, you should have seen her apartment… stripped bare. That's a lot of theatrics to try to trick me into stirring up votes from 'bottom dwellers'." When she said nothing, he continued. "And for what? To have an agenda that's pro-upper floors? Then why run against Fairchild… a guaranteed vote in favor of whatever Burke is trying to push through?"

Her pacing slowed. He watched the silhouettes of her hands rubbing palms against each other. She was thinking, and even that, he thought, she couldn't do without her body raising some kind of friction. Each hand seemed to be trying to outdo the other, trying to rub its opposite out of existence.

"There could be something there," she offered, her voice reluctant.

He nodded. "Of course, we have to get the word out to support her." He sat up, despite the spike of pain in his gut. "We can't do this alone, Dagmar."

"I've always done things alone."

It sounded to Crowe more like a lament than a determined stance.

"The Trust is falling apart," she said. "We're losing members by the day. Only the few who trust my militancy are staying. Others are forming their own factions, and some of them make me look soft by comparison."

His face flushed. He could feel the heat in his battered cheeks. "You have to get them back. You have to keep them in check. If they keep going after tenants or delivery people—if there's violence or vandalism—we won't get anywhere."

She came to the chair and sat again. "That's where you're part of the problem, Crowe."

"What?"

She slammed her fist into the mattress. "As our voice, as our messaging arm… you're not speaking what's in their hearts. The articles you're publishing in STORIES are so wishy-washy. Your words aren't matching their rage for what could happen if everything keeps going as it has been. People are getting to a point where they aren't going to take things anymore." She paused. "At least some people are." She went on. "Most of the Trust are just angry people who've been stepped on and forgotten too long. I don't know if they want to save the building as much as they want to lash out at something. I can't contain that forever."

His body sizzled with pain from flinching when she struck the bed. I *am* a coward, he thought.

"I can get them back… back before they do something that can't be retracted. But," she said, pointing a darkened finger at him, the point of the nail reflecting the limited available light of the room, "we have to give them something. News of what happened to you today will spread. If it goes unanswered, unretaliated, I can't make any promises about what they might do on their own."

"You think they care that much about me? You think—"

"No, damnit. It's not about caring about you or you at all. It's an excuse. What happened to you might as well just have happened to all of them. They are ready to strike."

He shook his head even as he understood that what she was saying was the inevitable truth. "It just can't be tied back to us, Dagmar." He grabbed her fist still sitting on the mattress and held it in place even as she tried to pull it away.

"Crowe?"

"Just…," he started, releasing her hand. "Just, let me think of something, before you do anything. Get the others to come back… promise them something big is coming. Something that will be a reckoning." He inhaled and then released it. "I'll think of something… God knows I'll have time lying in this bed."

"I can buy you a couple of days, at most, I think."

He nodded. "That's all I need, but nothing until then. Nothing."

She stood up. "I'm going to have somebody posted outside your door for the next couple of nights. Those men won't be back to bother you, and if they do come back, they'll find a fight."

She opened the door, all the more a silhouette, backlit by the light outside his bedroom door.

"Dagmar?" His wheels were turning.

She turned.

"Who do you think they were… those men?"

She speculated that they were probably from the Delivery Guild. "You're threatening their jobs. If deliveries dry up, they don't work."

He nodded. "But I think that's what someone wants me to think… wants us to think."

She told him to continue.

"It doesn't make sense. First, they called me Chicken Licken—"

"Jesus Christ, Crowe."

"No," he said, "hear me out. It's like maybe they were coached on a script, and they only half-listened to the training. I mean, for all of my fliers and canvassing, I doubt I've done much to slow down deliveries. But I might have put a small dent in someone's profit margin. Whose is the question?"

She crossed her arms and leaned against the doorjamb.

He told her if she wanted to, she should go to the stairwell right at that moment. "Just listen," he said. "You'll hear the endless drone of those delivery trucks coming up the access ramp. It's the drone the Delivery Guild has been complaining about. And no, not because they give a fig about the fate of this building. It's the work." He nodded, putting the ideas together in his head only a moment before releasing them to her. "Round-the-clock deliveries. Skeleton crew. Bad pay. No compensation if they pull a muscle or get a hernia." He pointed at her. "And then, just three months ago, the Board voted in the policy that the delivery crew couldn't accept tips." He slapped his hands together. "Even the wording of that motion… I mean, why not just vote that tenants can't tip? Why? Because that makes the Board and the tenants look cheap and callous. Instead, vote that delivery folks can't accept tips." He shrugged his hands in the air and then mimicked the voice of a complicit tenant. "'I'd like to tip, but I don't want to get them in trouble, right? I mean sure, if the Board told me I couldn't tip, I'd do it anyway, but the pressure is on them not to accept tips. I'm not going to tempt them. That wouldn't be very Christian of me.'"

Dagmar laughed.

He reveled for a moment in the idea of having drawn an emotion from her other than anger. "No, the delivery crew isn't worried about losing their jobs," he said. "Those men weren't from the Guild. At least I have a hard time believing that they were."

"Then who?"

"That I don't know. The tycoons? Hell, maybe even some board members get kickbacks on each sale. Maybe that's why some of them always vote against putting a limit on monthly deliveries."

"You might be onto something," she admitted.

"Yeah, well, it's giving me an idea." The synapses firing in his brain seemed to mask the pain enflaming his body. "Can you find out what you can about the President of the Delivery Guild... if there's anything questionable there?"

She said she would try.

"Good. Just anything that looks dirty."

She nodded. Then, she lingered in the doorway for a moment. "I remember you, you know."

He looked at her framed in the threshold of his bedroom. "You remember me?"

She nodded again. "You wouldn't have remembered me. I was a few grades behind you... pretty forgettable at the time."

"I doubt that. I'm sure you were—"

She crossed her arms. "Harvey Crochet. Remember that?"

Just hearing it gave him a chill. He was mocked with that name for years. He could still hear them: "Harvey Crochet! Harvey Crochet!" A classmate's mother had come in during second grade to show them crocheting. He'd made the mistake of sitting cross-legged on the floor, of raising his hand and asking her what someone would need to get started in such a hobby. He'd been genuinely curious and then paid for it for years. "Harvey Crochet! Harvey Crochet! Won't fight back, just runs away!"

"I had my bullies too, you know," Dagmar said. "I didn't exactly come from a lot of money. My clothes showed it. Sometimes I smelled of it during the times our water was shut off." She shook her head. "It made me an easy target."

"I'm sorry. That's rough. Believe me."

"Oh, I know. I watched you. The teasing, the beat downs. And I saw the way you just took it when you didn't run. That was right around the time my classmates were starting to notice how I didn't fit in either. In the early grades they didn't care, but by second grade the herd started to hone in on the odd-man-out that was me."

"Yes, that's when it started for me."

She waved her hand through the air violently. "I'm not trying to commiserate with you. I'm telling you, I watched you. And I promised myself sure as hell that wasn't going to be me." She crossed her arms again. "Later in second grade, I got lice. And this kid, Jack Currin… shit, I still remember his name. He starts calling me Lice Girl. And you know, that shit sticks. I listened to them for about a week. Went home every day crying. But then I thought of you." She shook her head. "No way that was going to be me. The next day I went to school, kicked Jack right in the sack, and dropped him to the ground. I told him if he ever called me Lice Girl again, he'd get it worse." She laughed. "Well, after school he wants to fight me, says I only got the upper hand because I sucker-kicked him." She shrugged. "I don't know, maybe I picked something up from watching my dad smack my mom around, but I let it all out on Jack. He didn't come back to school for two days. That didn't end it, though. The name-calling, that is. It kept up and I kept letting the rage out. By the end of that year, I'd fought half the kids in my class. By the third grade, I had no problems."

Crowe lay in the bed, his shame washing over him like a cold draft. "Wow. I sometimes wonder if I had just—"

"Wait. Let me finish."

He looked at her or at least the likeness of her in the shadow, arms crossed.

"They did leave me alone. Completely alone. I was shunned. All that fighting didn't win me admiration, just ostracization. I lost track of you after that. You were always just far enough ahead. When I moved into middle school, you were in the high school rooms. It wasn't until my freshman year that I saw you again. You were a senior and you had friends, people who talked to you and any trace of Harvey Crochet was gone. I was still lonely Lice Girl, even if nobody dared call me that."

He sat up a bit in the bed. "Well, I mean, I tutored some of—"

She held up a single finger to silence him some more. "It doesn't matter what you did. You did something different than me. For all my toughness, I didn't have a single friend." She put her arm back at her side. "So I'm just saying… don't always take what I say to heart. What do I know? I mean, why the hell do you think I recruited you after your parents died? The cause was going nowhere. I knew we needed smart people… people who were good with other people. People who were good with words." She pinched the bridge of her nose and then looked toward him again. "So, you know, don't go beating yourself up over the past. You've done enough of that. Me, I can get out of line sometimes. Like anything else—like knowing how to use a pencil like a knife—I know how to turn my mouth into a weapon." She put her hand on the doorknob.

"Hey, Dagmar?"

She paused.

"I'm your friend. You have a friend."

She stood a moment. "I know you are. I just don't know a lot about having one. You'll have to forgive me when I say the wrong things."

"It's okay," he said, but she'd closed the bedroom door, mumbling about having to use his shower before she left. It dawned on him that he hadn't felt any pain since she'd started confessing. Had that been his chance too to confess his feelings for her? He decided it wasn't, and his mind went back to its planning.

"Anya!"

Crowe rolled his eyes. He imagined the agony of getting out of bed to stuff a towel over the vent.

"Anya, I'm sorry. I shouldn't have taken your food. I really am sorry."

Crowe tried to see the vent, but couldn't. It was just a single, sorrowful voice coming out of the darkness of the corner.

The super's wife said nothing.

"Anya, I want to move the tape. I want you to have more of the apartment."

Nothing. Then: "Why? Because I'm so fat?"

"No, darling. I just want you to have it."

Crowe listened.

"Okay," she said. "I forgive you."

"Oh, darling… oh my, Anya."

Then there was something he'd never heard before. Giggling.

Crowe set his head back on the pillow and closed his eyes. He tried to put his plan together, but the sound of the shower took his mind elsewhere… imagining Dagmar in various stages of undressing, of the water washing over her, and then his foolish jealousy of the water itself.

CHAPTER 6

They huddled in the rec room on the 25th floor. Crowe checked the time. It was almost three o'clock in the morning. There were eleven other people, all members of ACT, waiting in the darkness with him. He could hear their breaths. He could smell the sweat wicking from their skin. The darkness felt like it had a pulse, and he heard it beating the same message: this is what should happen, this is what could happen, this is what should happen, this is what could happen, this is what should happen, this is what could happen…

"Remember," he said to the people he could feel, smell and hear, but not see, "nobody gets hurt."

Did they even respect him enough to listen? When they gathered in his apartment and he'd laid out the plan, had their rapt attention just been gaslighting? Sure, their faces said, we pretend to listen to Harvey Crochet now, and then we get our reward later: violence and mayhem. He'd made them empty anything that could be used as a weapon onto his kitchen table, though they only really paid attention to the demand when Dagmar insisted. "You pony up everything now, voluntarily," she'd said, "or I conduct a strip search that leaves you shitting as if you overdosed on laxatives." When they were done, the top of the table was covered with switchblades, brass knuckles, butterfly knives, a length of chain, pepper spray, nightsticks, and an assortment of pocket knives. Crowe had stared at the casual armory in disbelief.

"To be fair," she'd said, "they didn't know what this meeting was about. Some of this is just what a person carries to survive downstairs."

Crowe had wondered why some had even joined the cause. Was it only the possibility that they might get to bash in a rich person's head? He took solace that not everyone had set a weapon on the table. He knew the cause also had the backing of some college students and a handful of scholars, but they were only suited for protests, writing, and handing out fliers. For what they were about to do, they needed the people in the room behind him, which was Crowe's greatest fear.

"This," he'd said, pointing to the arsenal of weapons on his table, "is how we lose. One tenant gets hurt and our cause is crushed. Nobody will be persuaded by thugs. Even if it feels like you're finally doing something, you're doing nothing. Well, in truth, you would be doing something… bringing down the building with each act of violence. Instead, we are gaining important allies. Influential tenants are listening to our messaging. We have a chance to save ourselves and everyone else, but it demands restraint and self-discipline."

He didn't remember if they'd been looking at him as he spoke or through him to an imagined staircase behind him covered in blood.

"Look at my face," he'd said, pointing to the bruises. "I was the one assaulted. I was outnumbered and beaten in my kitchen.

I woke on the floor to the sight of my blood dried on the linoleum. If I can keep my cool, so can you."

The nods they'd given in return seemed obligatory. Enough with the words, their faces seemed to say.

"Nobody gets hurt," he repeated into the dark rec room. The space felt haunted by wrathful spirits, as though the meeting in his kitchen had been a séance that had summoned them.

He crouched for what felt like an eternity in that breathing, bated darkness. The air was damp and warm with the people around him. Their respiration became a single rhythm, and it gave him hope that their thoughts, like their breaths, were of one accord.

"Shh," Crowe hissed, hearing the footsteps in the hallway. He watched and, as he hoped, a man in a Delivery Guild uniform went past, dragging his feet, whistling tunelessly.

The room rustled around him.

"Not yet," Crowe whispered. "Stay back." He crawled to the doorway and peeked his head out.

At the end of the hallway, near the entrance to the Receiving Bay, Dagmar, draped in a vagrant's blanket, leaned against the wall pretending to sleep.

The delivery man stopped his half-hearted lope in front of her. He studied her as though he was deciding if he should do anything. After a moment, he nudged her with his foot. "Hey."

She pretended to stir and then looked up at him.

He shrugged his hands in the air in front of him apologetically. "You can't sleep here. You know that."

With the blanket still wrapped around her, she stood slowly. "Sorry."

He shrugged his shoulders. "Up to me, I'd let you sleep, but I've seen it get ugly when security guards find people dozing in the hallways."

Crowe turned and whispered into the room. "Did you hear that? These people are not the enemy. They're just the working stiffs." He felt them moving toward the doorway behind him. He rose slowly to his feet, sensing the bottled energy gathering around him ready to explode.

"Stick to the plan," he said.

Stepping away from Dagmar, the delivery man punched in some numbers on a keypad. When the door opened, Dagmar looped the blanket around him, pinning his arms to his side. Her unveiling revealed that she was also wearing a delivery uniform.

"Hey!"

"Stay quiet," she growled in his ear.

The group following Crowe out of the rec room were also wearing older delivery uniforms that some ACT members had salvaged from the Refuse Bay.

Dagmar pushed the man into the door, opening it the rest of the way. Crowe and the others followed her inside and quickly closed the door behind them.

So far, so good.

The Receiving Bay was enclosed with a ceiling high enough to allow delivery trucks to enter from the access ramp. A driverless truck had already passed through the PVC strip door that hung over the entrance like the tentacles of an enormous, transparent squid. As Crowe expected, it was being offloaded before ever setting a tire on the scale plate.

Dagmar pushed her captive against the wall and twisted the blanket tight behind him. Then, she turned him around so he faced the bay. "Not a goddamn word," she said, sticking a finger in his face.

Through his fear, his puzzled eyes examined her delivery uniform.

The other ACT members had dashed for the truck and overpowered the man and woman unloading it. The overnight shifts always only had a skeleton crew.

"Nobody gets hurt!' Crowe shouted.

"They know!" Dagmar hissed back at him. "Just get to it." She motioned with a thrust of her head toward the man pinned against the wall. His eyes were wide with alarm. Get to what? they seemed to ask.

Crowe stepped in front of him. The man's face was pale. His brow broke out with sweat. "Look, we aren't going to hurt anyone. Okay?" Crowe arched his eyebrows. "Okay?"

After a moment, the man nodded.

Crowe looked over his shoulder. The other two delivery people, seated against the wall, were now tied up too. They were still wearing their respirators and looked unharmed. Their heads rotated around as they watched the activity.

Crowe turned back to the trembling man. "See? Nobody's getting hurt. Just take it easy. There's something you need to know. Okay?" He waited.

The man nodded. "Okay."

"Your guild president, Jake Harsmith, is a grifter. So are your floor stewards. You've been getting played." He explained that Dagmar's people had pretty sound evidence that Harsmith and others were on the take.

The man shook his head. "Can't be. Not Harsmith."

"Shut up."

Crowe flashed Dagmar a look. She put her hand up as an apology.

"Ok, sorry," she said. "But just listen. This isn't made up."

Behind him, Crowe could hear the rapid deflation of the truck tires. He looked. "Goddamn it, Dagmar. We said no weapons."

Still pressing the man to the wall, she glanced behind her and then turned to Crowe. "They're not weapons. They're utility knives. Let them have a little fun."

"Tires only," he said through clenched teeth. He turned back to the man. "Some members of the Board are paying Harsmith and the shop stewards to keep you guys gaslit. Plain and simple, they're lying to you. Everything you're hearing is to keep you afraid for your jobs." He explained what the Board received in return: A low payout to the delivery crew. No need to pay overtime. No sick leave. No safety equipment for heavy deliveries. Fudged weight readings."

The man shook his head.

"No? Then why is that truck ready to be offloaded, but it's nowhere near the scale?"

The man looked at the semi-truck sheepishly.

"You can talk," Crowe said.

"Harsmith said if too much weight comes into the building, there'll be restrictions, and we'll lose our jobs."

Dagmar laughed. "If too much weight comes into the building, this sonuvabitch is going to drop like—"

"Dagmar."

Her nostrils flared, but she went quiet.

Crowe squeezed the man's shoulder as though he were a friend. "Look, Harsmith is working for the Board, or at least for Burke, and he's getting paid for it. He's sharing some with the shop stewards, and they're working their crews to death. It's all about money and—" Crowe leaped at the sound of shattering glass. He turned to see one of their members, a tall dark-skinned man, with a plasma television up over his head. "Stop!"

The man sent the television careening down into the shards of aquarium glass scattered over the floor.

Crowe marched across the unloading dock, planted his hands into the man's chest, and slammed him against the side of the truck.

"What in the hell are you doing?!"

The man looked down, taking a moment to register that it was Crowe who had manhandled him. His brows knit together.

"You said to."

"What?"

"You said, if we found anything addressed to Harsmith or Burke, we should smash it." He explained that the aquarium was addressed to Burke and the television to Harsmith.

Crowe backed off from the man, holding his hands in the air in exasperation. It was true. He'd told them to do that. That it would send a message. He never would have guessed that they both would have had a delivery on the same truck.

"That's right, I did say that. I'm sorry."

The man rubbed his back where it had hit the side of the truck. Half of his mouth rose into a little smile. "Thought you said nobody gets hurt."

Crowe nodded. “I know. I’m sorry.” He squeezed his forehead in his hand. “Just finish up.” He looked into the man’s bearded face. “I do apologize.”

He walked back over to the delivery man Dagmar still had pinned against the wall. Her grin damned Crowe and praised him at the same time. “Well, look at you,” she said. “Harvey Crowbar. I worried we might have some hotheads tonight, but this is unexpected.”

“Just stop.” He turned his attention back to his captive audience.

“I’ve heard about you. You’re Chicken Little,” the man said.

He shook his head. “No, I’m Harvey Crowe, and I want you to remember my name. Got it?” He took a moment and spelled out his last name for him. “With an ‘e’.”

The man nodded.

“Say it,” Dagmar demanded.

“Harvey Crowe, with an ‘e’.”

“Now look,” Crowe started, “the Guild has a lot more power than you’ve been led to believe. You’ve been told you’re at the mercy of the work, which is merciless.” He pointed at the man’s heart. “But the reality is that the profits are at your mercy. If these deliveries stop, rich folks are going to lose a ton of money.” Behind him, he heard the back door of the truck slam down, and then the swivel and thunk of the lock assembly. The hiss of spray paint cans followed. Almost done, he thought. “When they ask, just say we were in delivery uniforms but wearing masks. And then you just watch what happens when you tell ‘em this. You watch. They’ve got you so wired with fear and doubt that you won’t even negotiate on your behalf.” He shook his head. “You’re paying dues to this guild, for god's sake! That's like running after a mugger to give him the money he missed in your front pockets."

Crowe touched his fingers along his bruised cheek. "You know my name if you or any of your brothers or sisters want to do anything about this. All I'm asking is you take a day or two and watch what happens when they find out." He looked at Dagmar. "Loosen the blanket knot a bit now."

Turning the man around, she went to work.

He turned and looked at the truck. Its tires were flattened and the sides had been spray-painted with slogans: Strike for shorter hours! Better pay! Tips!

One of the ACT members walked over to a control panel, pressed a green button, and the truck's engine started up. It trundled forward on its flattened tires and disappeared through the plastic departure doors. Crowe listened to the outside hermetic door rise along its tracks, pause, and then come back down again. Those closest to the doorway held their breath until the heavy plastic flapped back into place.

He looked at the man one more time. "Just watch," he said. "You're going to see changes." He swallowed. "I hope."

The ACT group reassembled briefly to a few high fives and then exited out into the main hallway. With no security guards in sight, they pushed open the fire door to the stairwell and sprinted down the steps, dispersing onto different floors, shedding delivery uniforms, and then stuffing them into wall chutes where they would slide down into the building's incinerator.

Crowe checked the time when he opened the door to his apartment. Half-past four in the morning. He stood for a moment with his hands on the back of a kitchen chair. He took a deep breath. It felt like his first in over two hours. Everything from the Receiving Bay replayed in his mind, but he seemed to recall it as if a dream he'd just woken from. The weapons scattered across his table told him otherwise.

We did it, he thought. Now, will it do anything?

He shivered. Having worn two layers of clothes, plus the running, not to mention the fear and sudden charges of adrenaline, he was soaked in sweat. He stripped off the remaining clothes on his way to the bedroom, letting them lie where they fell. He collapsed into his bed naked and pulled the blankets up to his neck. Later in the afternoon, he'd have time to think about everything that had happened… time to hope for the results they needed. At that moment, he just wanted to sleep.

"Oh, Sam."

The super's wife's voice drifted out of the vent. She sounded on the verge of weeping.

Do they ever sleep? Crowe wondered, pounding the back of his head into his pillow.

But it wasn't weeping. She was chortling.

"Sam! You're a wolf! A hungry, naughty wolf."

"Anya, I've missed you this way."

They had reached a détente, or soon were going to. Even if it wasn't their usual arguing or screaming, Crowe knew he couldn't sleep through it. With foresight, he'd started keeping a towel in his bedroom to cover the vent. If he left the vent covered all the time, the room was either too hot or too cold and stuffy with stale air. He closed his eyes and shook his head from side to side. He sighed breathily. The towel was across the room on the dresser – only eight feet, but may as well have been the length of one of the building's 1500-foot hallways for how tired he felt.

Moments later, he heard the door to his apartment opening. He listened again, hoping he'd misheard, but sure enough, he heard it quietly closing. The latch slipped into the strike plate. Whoever it was locked the door again. Had he been so intoxicated with what they'd done that he'd left the door unlocked? He thought of the tabletop of weapons that he'd left for his would-be assailants. They certainly had their range of choices. Footsteps crept down the hallway toward his bedroom. His heart started up as though being worked like a speed bag. Icy inertia shot through his veins.

It struck him suddenly. He'd been wrong. The men who had beaten him four nights before must have been from the Delivery Guild. They'd told him to stop causing problems. What did he do in response? Nothing much… just lead a group of agitators to the Receiving Bay, tied up their co-workers, smashed merchandise, vandalized a truck, and made it look like it had been done by delivery workers. And, of course, he'd told them his name. Even spelled it for them. Their last visit had left him in bed for nearly twenty-four hours. Would he even live through this one?

He sat up but realized his clothes were scattered from his kitchen to his room. Even his underwear was just inside his bedroom's threshold.

"Sam, Sam, Sam… Sam!"

The pounding of his heart matched that of the super's climaxing wife. He balled his hands into fists. He would fight.

"Crowe?"

Absently, his hand rose and touched its fingertips along his lips. "Dagmar?"

As she had before, she was standing there, a silhouette framed in his bedroom door.

"Hey," she said, "I couldn't sleep."

He blinked. A metallic taste filled his mouth. "How did you get in here?"

"You gave me a key a long time ago."

She was right. He had. He swallowed. "You're having a hard time sleeping?"

She leaned into the doorframe. "After something like that, I'm always too wired for sleep. Like I have this energy that I can't shake. It's like restless legs, but all over."

"Do… do you want to talk?"

"No." She reached down, arms crossed at the wrists, and then lifted her t-shirt over her head, revealing the stretch of her torso, the outline of her breasts.

Crowe swallowed again. "I…"

She walked across the room and pulled the covers off of him. Seeing him naked she smiled. "I guess maybe you were waiting for me?"

He scratched his head. "I guess maybe so."

She took his hands and put them on her waistband. His fingers, having more instinct than him, popped open the button and unzipped the teeth of her fly. The backs of his fingers brushed against the soft downy skin just beneath her navel. It sent a chill right through him.

"Crowe?"

"I'm okay." He watched her shimmy out of her pants. "Dagmar, I just wanted to say—"

"You're going to ruin this, aren't you?"

He closed his mouth.

She pushed him back onto the bed, straddled him, and soon they were drowning out any of the sounds coming from the vent.

When he woke, it was to something rustling the mattress. He opened his eyes. Facing the wall, he saw the usual gray coming through his frosted window. Then he remembered and rolled over. Already dressed, Dagmar was sitting on the edge of the bed. She lifted a leg and pulled a sock up over her toes and then her foot. He smelled her scent—a faint hint of gasoline—still on the pillow.

"Good morning, beautiful."

She turned and looked at him, giving him a quick smile. "Morning." She turned back to the task of the other sock. "And don't call me that."

He reached out and touched her back, but the way she flinched made him pull his hand away.

"Everything okay?"

She remained turned away from him. "Everything's fine."

"You sure? Do you want to come back to bed?"

She stood up and faced him, fully dressed, aside from her boots. "It's late. I want to hear if there's any news after last night."

"What time is it?"

"Almost four."

He repeated the time she'd said. He shook his head. "I don't think I've slept that well in a long time."

"Sex will do that."

He studied her. "You sure everything is okay?"

She stood a moment hovering over him. "Jesus Christ, Crowe, we fucked, that's all. You're not going to ask me to marry you now, are you?"

Sitting up, he exhaled and threw off the covers.

She turned away swiftly. "Oh my god, put some clothes on."

Sitting on the edge of the bed, he pulled the sheet over his lap. "Dagmar, I just think we should talk about—"

"You are going to ruin this, aren't you? Just… fine, it didn't happen, okay?" She marched out of the room. "I'm going to find out if there's any buzz." She opened the door to his apartment. "I'm sorry for… just… I'll see you later," she called.

"Okay," he shouted.

He imagined her grabbing her boots and walking out into the hallway in just her socks. At least she'd attempted to apologize. He knew enough about psychology to register the significance of her mentioning an abusive father. Watching her mother and father in a toxic relationship would have established for her that putting your trust in anyone is dangerous business.

He dressed slowly, his mind replaying the hours they had spent together. Stunned by the developments and not wanting to do or say anything that might jinx them, he had been uncharacteristically quiet. When she had spoken, it was always the same question: "You think you're ready to go again?" He remembered at times it had felt more like watching somebody have sex the way she engaged with such disconnection. When they'd finally decided to sleep, she rolled away from his embrace, making his tiny mattress feel king-sized by the distance she was able to make. And still, it was the most connected he'd felt to someone in years. He wondered what that said about his psychology. Is that all he felt he deserved?

He walked into his kitchen and quickly collected the tabletop full of weapons into a towel. He set them carefully in a drawer as though they might be radioactive. He hoped they would be gone by that evening.

Near the door, he spotted a package and an envelope. Dagmar must have taken them from his hallway box and set them inside. At least she'd done that. He knew the package was just his meager weekly grocery delivery. He opened the envelope and found fliers regarding Mrs. Montgomery's campaign for a board seat.

He sat at his kitchen table and read through the flier. There was no other note. Had she come all the way down to the 9th floor to deliver them? Who else would she have entrusted with the task? He tried to imagine her descending the staircase… the risk she was taking considering the rampant rumors of stairwell crimes on the lower levels. Of course, in her position, it would have been easy to ride down on one of the service elevators. She could have easily told an elevator attendant that she was delivering a care package as some of the upper floor folks were sometimes inclined to do. "My husband just passed away," he imagined her saying. "I have some of his socks in here I thought someone could use." Whatever means she'd used, he admired her bravery.

Regardless, reading through the flier, he wasn't sure what she expected him to do with the nearly 200 copies she'd sent. The language didn't speak at all to the needs of those on the lowest floors. Then again, how could it? If someone from the Fairchild campaign smelled even a whiff of pro-lower messaging, her bid for a seat would be sunk, widow or no. He guessed the fliers would at least be name recognition for her. Fairchild was largely despised among the 'bottom dwellers', so knowing that there was an alternative might get some to vote for her, if they voted at all.

He looked for his satchel, but then remembered that it'd been stolen. He stuffed the fliers back into the envelope. Taking a knife from the silverware drawer, he picked up the grocery package. Turning it in his hands, he discovered someone had written in marker on the bottom:

WE ARE WATCHING.

He threw the box to the table, as though he suddenly realized it was a snapping turtle and not a package at all. He took deep breaths. Was it a threat? But then why make a threat? Why not just kick in his door and then kick in his head? He snapped his fingers. No, that's what he'd said. "Just watch... just watch what happens." They, like he and Dagmar, were just waiting and watching to see if anything would come of the operation from the night before. He pictured what they'd done—what he'd done!—and like recalling his fornication with Dagmar, it felt more like something he'd witnessed than experienced. Had that been him... slamming a man nearly twice his size against the side of a truck? Yes, he thought, that was me. And so, there were many in a state of waiting and watching for something that could go marvelously right or catastrophically wrong. Either way, there was no doubt that *they* knew where he lived.

The realization of his ravenous hunger shook him from his speculating. His stomach felt hollow, as though he hadn't eaten in days. He cut open the grocery package and, though he would have normally saved them for later in the week, he took out the packet of vacuum-sealed soy beef tips and began to rehydrate them in a frying pan. Normally, he'd divide the package into quarters, using the "meat" to help season servings of rice or noodles. Instead, he dumped the entire package into a half cup of simmering Just Like Water. Then he devoured them. A night with Dagmar had been good for his sleep, but it turned out it was equally good for his appetite.

Stabbing up the last of the dull gray morsels, he thought of her again and wanted to be with her again. But even through his desire, he felt his longing for it to be something more, and also the realization that such longing was just fantasy, like longing to see a dead relative after having a fleeting dream about them the night before.

Crowe later met with his students in the recreation room on the 22nd floor. The need for his tutoring had grown to such an extent that rather than meeting one-on-one in their apartments, he was meeting with all of them. He'd arranged tables by grades and navigated around the room helping with the specific questions that they couldn't answer together.

"You have to try to teach each other," he repeated. "Don't be dependent on me. You're smart. And we are in this together." He prowled between the tables. "When people encounter a problem, it's best to admit that there's a problem, see the scope of the problem, and act collectively to solve the problem." Now and again, a student would give him a look as if to say, "We are just talking about homework, right?" With a smile, he'd point the student's attention back to the work on the table.

The parents of his students had expanded beyond security guards, including a handful of students from the upper floors. They came with pockets of cash of which Crowe only took a small amount. Some left after realizing that even if offered enough money, Crowe wouldn't tutor them one-on-one exclusively. For those that stayed, he took an amount that seemed fair which allowed him to offer the supervised group study sessions for free to the others. As much as he wanted to offer it free to all of them, a recent accounting of his personal funds had shown him that he needed some kind of income coming in.

One of the parents, a plumber in the building, had found a storage room with a dusty chalkboard on wheels tucked in the far corner. She'd retrieved it and brought it to the rec room when Crowe had said he could use it for teaching. He'd wheel it around the room working out math problems, outlining essays, illustrating battlefields, and demonstrating chemistry solutions. When he could, he'd call a student to the board to let them teach the others.

He tried to focus as much as he could on the teachings. Still, his mind would drift uneasily.

"Mr. Crowe?"

He looked down at the fresh face of a fourth-grader pointing her finger at the door. A person he didn't recognize stood in the doorway watching the activity. She was smiling. Making sure the students were busy, he excused himself and went over to greet the visitor. She wore her red hair pulled up into a loose bun. He admitted to himself that she was attractive. He brushed his chalk-dusted fingers on his sleeve.

"You're good," she said as he got closer.

He nodded. "Thank you. They make it easy with their enthusiasm." He shook her hand and then cleared his throat. "This isn't to be rude, but I usually ask that parents don't linger. I think the students are more relaxed if—"

"I'm not a parent," she said, shaking her head. "I teach 7th grade history down on the 20th floor school."

"Oh," he said. "Well, I want you to know that I'm making them do all of their own work."

"I know," she said. She pointed at two boys at the 7th grade study table. "Those two are mine: Luke and Tim. A month ago I couldn't get anything out of them. Now they won't stop talking… but in the best way possible." She said she believed it was because of him.

He smiled. "I'm sure I've got it easier working with them in small groups like this. I couldn't imagine trying to teach a room full of 30."

She chuckled. "Try 50."

He shook his head. "Amazing the things that get prioritized over education."

She nodded. "I do think you're being modest, though. You're a natural teacher. Have you ever thought about it?"

He shrugged. "Maybe at one time. Somehow though, I ended up in marketing."

"Mr. Crowe, are we learning or dating?" a senior student shouted. "I have a math exam tomorrow."

Some in the room tittered into their hands at the comment.

"Oooh…Ms. Simmons and Mr. Crowe sparking some heat," Luke shouted and then quickly ducked his head back to his book.

Crowe felt his face flush. "I…"

She smiled. "I should let you get back to your work. It doesn't take much to lose them." She held out her hand. "Sarah Simmons."

He took her chilled grip. Was she nervous too? "Harvey Crowe. It is good to meet you." He turned back to the kids. "Alright, alright… let's get back to it."

"We never stopped, Mr. Crow-meo."

The kids laughed again.

He pointed at the eighth-grader, her face a wide smile. "I'll allow that because it's a grade-appropriate Shakespeare reference." In his college days, Crowe had written a paper regarding *Romeo and Juliet*, arguing that the true tragedy—and the subsequent cause of the young lovers' tragedy—was the weak Prince.

The Prince was adept at making threatening speeches: "If ever you disturb our streets again, your lives shall pay the forfeit of the peace." But Crowe pointed out that this was after three street brawls had already occurred between the Montagues and Capulets. Later, when Mercutio is slain, rather than carry out his idle threat from earlier in the play, the Prince talks about the heavy fine that he will amerce. What would this "heavy fine" mean to such affluent families? Nothing. The true victims were the citizens of Verona who had to live in the chaos of the prideful feuding of the privileged few.

"It is this weak leadership," the young Crowe had written, "that fails to govern in times that warrant governance that is the sole cause of the play's tragedy. What if the Prince had made more than empty threats and rulings? How was it that these wealthy families had fought in the streets of Verona 'thrice' and yet nothing had been done?"

Crowe had written about how the Prince had ended his long speech at the beginning by saying, "You Capulet; shall go along with me:/And, Montague, come you this afternoon." He speculated in his essay that this was the prelude to a backroom deal that surely would benefit all three parties—the Prince turning a blind eye to the violence of the younger members of the families and in turn his majesty receiving their continued political support.

If the Prince, Crowe had argued, had taken a hard line and forced a house arrest on the families until their feud was ended, there would be no tragedy in the tragedy of Romeo and Juliet.

Maybe it would have truly been a love story. "Sadly, the Prince is an ineffective leader with unenforced rules and lengthy diatribes about the penalty such behavior will elicit. Given the wealth of the Montagues and the Capulets, one can only conclude that the Prince is beholden to them, and their money speaks louder than his rules or his concern for the citizenry, hence his ineffectual leadership. The Prince's sense of justice and the need to govern for the common good was overshadowed by his fecklessness in the face of the families' wealth and opulence."

The essay had earned a B-. To his last sentence, his professor had written in the margins: "speculation!" Much of the rest of the paper, in the teacher's words, was "a stretch." He had pointed out that Crowe's argument focused entirely too much on a minor character who barely appears in the play. And the young Crowe had thought, "But isn't his lack of appearances his very failure as a leader? How does one know about brawling and sword fights in the streets, and yet does nothing?" In hindsight, the grade he'd been given was justified academically. Much of the paper was speculation, as well as verbose and repetitive. At the time, though, he thought it worthy of publication. He smiled at the audacity of his younger self; he had always been a dreamer.

When Crowe looked up again from his musings, it was Dagmar standing in the doorway, leaning into the doorjamb much the way she had the night before in his bedroom. Was she smiling as she watched him work with the children and what, he thought, did that smile mean? Was she thinking about the night they'd spent together? Was he the reason for her smile? Or, did she see an effeminate man tending to children like a nanny? With her, he could never tell.

Crowe walked over to her.

"Oof! Mr. Crowe sure is a player!" one of the kids shouted.

He turned back to them. "Never mind that, get back to your work."

"What was that about?" she asked.

He smiled. "Nothing. It must be you. You look beautiful."

She shook her head. "I told you not to say that."

"Say what?"

She crossed her arms. "Listen, I haven't heard anything. I don't know if that's good or bad."

Crowe thought for a moment. "I don't either."

"I've got ears on it, but they're hearing nothing."

He shrugged. "It's a waiting game, I guess."

She looked around the room. "When are you done here?'

He told her he still had about twenty minutes.

"Okay, I'll see you later." She looked into his face. "And stop looking at me like that."

"Like what?"

She shook her head and stomped out into the hallway.

"Dagmar?"

When he leaned through the doorway to look after her, he could almost feel the cold she'd left behind. He turned back to look into the room at the kids. They were working well, teaching each other, sometimes laughing. All this life going on, he thought, in the shadow of calamity, visions of the building's collapse materializing in his mind's eye. It was the children that spared him from his own dark prophesizing, calling him back with their questions or their sudden understanding of a concept. Live in the moment, he thought and he returned to his task of helping his young subjects.

At around nine o'clock, he and Dagmar were sitting in his kitchen. He was at the stove fixing them noodles. He felt the guilt at having eaten all of the beef tips, something that he could have added as a little treat, a little flavor, to the bland meal he was preparing. "I'm sorry I don't have more to offer," he said.

"I'm not hungry." She muttered restlessly. She'd sit for a moment at the table balling her hands into fists and then suddenly splay her fingers out wide. Then, just as suddenly, she'd stand and pace like the caged wolves he'd seen in an ancient zoo on a historical documentary he'd watched.

A knock sounded at the door.

She looked at Crowe. "Where are those knives?"

He held up his hands to her and pumped them calmingly. "Just relax." He walked toward the door. "They're in the top drawer."

Dagmar moved to the counter and leaned against it, her hand resting on the drawer pull.

Crowe squinted his eye to the peephole. A shudder went through him. Three men were standing, their fisheye faces looking pensive.

"Three guys," he whispered. "But not the guys that showed up here the other night." From what he could tell, they weren't wearing delivery uniforms. "I'm not sure who they are."

They knocked again, louder.

Dagmar pulled the drawer open and let her hand hover above its dangerous cache. "Might as well do it."

Crowe took a long breath and exhaled before raising his hand to the deadbolt. When it clicked, he braced himself, expecting that they'd just rush the door at the sound.

He opened the door. Out of the distortion of the peephole's glass, Crowe's eyes registered that one of them was the guy Dagmar had tied up with her blanket.

"Hello?"

"We watched," the man said, nodding.

Crowe tried to gauge their demeanor. Their faces gave nothing away.

"Can we come in?"

He nodded, opening the door wider and gesturing for them to enter. They sat at Crowe's small kitchen table. One of the men accepted a plate of noodles and spun them up on his fork. The guy from the Receiving Bay introduced himself as Ricky.

"Sorry I didn't make introductions last night." He looked at Dagmar. "I wasn't in a position to shake hands."

In response, she smiled and closed the drawer.

Ricky explained that the Board had called an emergency closed-door meeting with the delivery personnel earlier that evening.

"What? My people are slipping," Dagmar mumbled.

Ricky looked at her and then back at Crowe. He shook his head. "I'm thinking, emergency meeting… that's it, they're shit-canning all of us for last night's stunt. While I was getting ready for the meeting, I just kept thinking, 'Harvey Crowe…

I'm going to get my severance pay out of that sonuvabitch in his blood."

Crowe swallowed.

"And so, we get there, and Harsmith is all somber and so are the shop stewards. And I'm like 'that's it, the bad news is coming.' Instead, though, they don't say much. They say we got a special guest, and then they introduce Chairman Burke."

"No shit," Dagmar whispered incredulously.

Looking at her, Ricky nodded. "So, Burke gets going on something about how much the Board appreciates the hard work of the guild. He says with other items like Operation Steel, they'd had to table a long-standing proposal to look at an updated cost-of-living package for the guild—"

"Bullshit."

Crowe looked at her. "Just listen, Dagmar."

She apologized and then reached up and turned an invisible key at her pursed lips. She then tossed the phantom key over her shoulder.

"So," Ricky says, "he lays it all out. Fifteen percent raise for all members. Round-the-clock delivery cut down to 12 hours a day. New safety gear. And the whole time behind them Harsmith and the shop stewards got looks on their faces like this is bad news. They were struggling to force smiles, but I'm guessing whatever is coming to us is coming out of their pockets, kickback-wise."

Crowe took it all in and exhaled a long breath. "So, it worked," he said.

Ricky nodded. "Guess we had 'em by the short hairs all along and just didn't know it." He explained that some of the guild members were scrambling to put up a candidate against Harsmith in the upcoming guild elections. "You should have seen Harsmith after Burke left. He was parading around up there like he had something to do with it… saying he'd been having meetings with the Board about our working conditions for some time. Nobody was buying it. The rumors of what went down on that Receiving Bay last night had spread through the guild pretty quickly."

"You played a part in that," Crowe said, "by being patient." He scratched behind his neck. "Have you given any thought to running for the president position?"

Ricky laughed. "That ain't me, man. We're thinking Jesse Southgate. She's got a head for it. Good talker too… even-keeled."

Crowe said that she sounded like a good choice.

"We owe you," Ricky said.

Crowe looked back at a smiling Dagmar still leaning against the counter. He turned back to his guests. "We're just happy it worked out and made a difference."

"Thanks for the noodles."

Crowe closed and then locked the door after the men left. When he turned, he saw Dagmar's t-shirt on the kitchen floor and her fingers working at the safety pin holding her bra strap together. She faded out into the darkness of the hallway that led to his bedroom. He went after her, flicking open the buttons on his shirt.

Afterward, he was woken by a strange sound. His first thought was that the super and his wife were at it again—the sounds of their reconciliation just as annoying as that of their aggressions. But, no. It was Dagmar lying next to him. Crying.

He reached out and set his hand on her shoulder. She let it stay.

"You okay?"

Her shoulders shook with her sobbing.

"Dagmar?"

"It's all wrong," she said.

"Hey," he said, panicked, "we don't even know what this is yet. I don't have any expectations that this—"

She wrenched her shoulder from under his hand and swung her legs over to sit on the edge of the bed. The bones of her spine popped out along her back as she leaned forward to put her face in her hands. "I'm not talking about us, goddamnit. There is no us."

He lay for a moment with his hand over his mouth. He sighed. "Then, what—"

"Where is my shirt?" She was bent fully over, her arms groping the floor in the darkness.

"It's in the kitchen. Just take mine."

Finding his, she stood with her back to him. She buttoned the shirt and then turned to him. "I just don't know, Crowe. I mean, what are we now… labor organizers? What the hell does any of this have to do with the building?"

He sat up and set his back against the wall, wrapping his arms around the knees drawn to his chest. "No. I—"

"We are running out of time!"

He knew what she was talking about. The building. The cracks. The load. And yet still, they couldn't celebrate a victory?

"We did a good thing," he said. "Our members needed some action. They got it. We have allies now in the Delivery Guild. That could come in handy. Plus, we helped them get better pay."

"Dead people don't spend their raises." She pointed at him. "Don't say anything. Just don't. I've looked at the numbers… well, as accurate as they are. They're probably worse. In best case scenario, this building has about nine months before it crushes itself under its weight. Worst case? Five months." She looked up at the ceiling. "What the hell are we even doing?"

He combed his fingers back through his sleep-matted hair. "Deliveries just went from 24 hours a day to 12 hours a day. You don't think that will—"

She was laughing.

"What?"

"Are you thick, Crowe? Do you think that won't just mean twice as many trucks coming up the ramp during the day?"

"Well…" He had nothing else. "We're trying."

She kicked along the floor in the darkness until she found her jeans. She pushed her foot into one of the pant legs, hopping on the other leg. "Are we? What's our direction? How do we offload—I don't know, what?—50 or 60 tons of weight? And what does that even buy us, an extra month or two? You and all the writing, all the words… how many minds has it changed?"

He said that it changed Mrs. Montgomery's mind. "That election is coming up soon."

She laughed. "What is that, Crowe? What is it?! Nothing. One voice that will be drowned out by the rest of those bastards eager to fill their coffers. It's 30 seconds to midnight, and you're celebrating some senile biddy that's seen the light."

"She's not senile." He scooted forward and sat on the edge of the bed. "What are you saying that you want to do?"

She zipped up her pants and closed the button. "I don't know, but not this. I mean, we showed we can do something. We showed that the Board can be scared. We just have to figure out how to use that energy."

"For what? Beat up some tenants? Break into some apartments, requisition the service elevator, and bring some stolen deep freezers down to the Refuse Bay?"

"I don't know!" she shouted.

"One wrong move and ACT is a pariah. Right now, we're an annoyance, and we're tolerated." He stood up and took her by both shoulders. "We screw this up, it's all lost."

She looked into his eyes, her own reflecting the caged wolf—eyes seeing things beyond seeing. "It's all lost, anyway." Planting her hands into his chest, she shoved him back onto the bed. "Just leave me alone."

She slammed the door behind her on the way out.

Crowe lay on the bed, his head pounding with ache. She was right. They were running out of time. In his head, he could hear the rumble. The start of it. And then fast, the whole thing coming down in an implosion of dust and lives.

Deaths.

"Anya, wake up, you're snoring like a Christmas pig." A moment passed. "Anya!"

"What, for chrissake?"

Crowe pulled the blanket up over his head. His tears were coming.

"I just need you to roll over, darling. I can't sleep."

"Then go to the other bed. I can't sleep on my side."

"Yes, you can! I've seen it! I'm just asking you to roll your fat ass on its side!"

"Get out, Sam! Get out!"

Crowe heard no more—all of it drown out by the gargle of his sobbing breaths. The image of it—all of it coming down—played in his head on a never-ending loop of disaster footage.

CHAPTER 7

Crowe stood in the freight elevator as it ascended rattling up its shaft. It stopped for delivery people who, upon seeing him, simply nodded. He was now well-known in their circles and admired for what he'd done to change their working conditions. When he'd asked Ricky about access to the elevator that morning, he'd only been met with, "How can I say no?" Unlike the guest elevators, there was no attendant. The other—the service elevator—was used exclusively by the maintenance department. Nobody but the delivery people would know of his stowaway status in the freight elevator. He patted his hand at his side, which was his habit, only to be reminded again that his satchel was gone.

The days since the Board's emergency closed-door session had been volatile. The other guilds had heard about the sudden change to the working conditions for the delivery personnel. The Maintenance Guild and the Security Guild had started rattling their sabers about the unfairness. The presidents of those guilds, likely loyal to Burke and the Board, did their best to keep their members calm. They explained what the delivery crew had endured for so long, but their members came back with details of their long hours, poor pay, and dangerous working conditions. There was talk of striking, and the talk was growing louder and more determined.

Even with the agitation in the guilds, Crowe had heard nothing from Dagmar. She'd stormed out of his apartment that night and had seemingly vanished. He kept his ears open for any stories about what ACT was up to, but he heard little. When he found a few of their members in the 6th floor rec room, they told him that they hadn't heard from or seen Dagmar either. Whether or not they were lying for her, he couldn't be sure. When he asked what they were doing in service to the cause, they simply said, "waiting." Though spoken softly enough, the one-word answer left an ominous feeling in the moldy air of the rec room.

The freight elevator hit the 57th floor and stopped. Crowe looked up and down the empty hallway. Board members' apartment numbers were kept as secret as could be, but Ricky was happy to tell him the information he wanted.

Walking toward his destination, he stopped and looked at himself in one of the hallway mirrors. He'd done his best to look presentable, though the results were passable at best. He had a shirt and tie that he'd worn for the rare video conference calls he had to make as a low-level marketer for Just Like Water. The shirt was wrinkled and yellowed under the arms. His pants, the same pants he'd worn for Leo's funeral, were frayed at the cuffs. Given the weight he'd lost since the death of his parents, he'd had to cut another hole in his belt to keep his pants from falling. That morning, he'd worked with scissors at his shaggy hair. The mirror in front of him showed the hair on the back of his neck, overgrown like weeds. Disappointed, he had turned from the glass, exasperated.

He stood for a moment in front of apartment 57-126. Then, he knocked. He waited for the video peephole to come online, but instead, the door opened directly. There stood LaMark with puzzled eyes. He was holding a cup of coffee with steam still drifting from its surface.

"Do you remember me?" Crowe asked.

LaMark looked him over cautiously. "I suppose. Maybe. What do you want?"

Crowe touched his cheek where he'd cut himself that morning trying to shave with a dull razor. "I wanted to talk with you about load-related issues with the building."

LaMark's face turned stern as he began to close the door.

"Board business is for board meetings."

"Sir?" Crowe reached out only to have his fingers caught between the closing door and the jamb. He stumbled back and fell against the opposite wall. The throbbing pain lowered him down to sitting where, eyes closed, he squeezed the wounded digits with the fingers of his other hand.

"Are you okay?"

He opened his eyes to see LaMark crouched down to his level. The kindness had returned to his face.

"Hmm? Let's take a look."

Crowe held his hand out in front of him gingerly opening and closing the fingers. "I don't think anything's broken."

LaMark carefully took the hand in his own. He turned it, examining the red line across the back of the fingers. "I'm sorry. I couldn't have known you would—"

"It's not your fault. I shouldn't be here at your home like this. I just don't know what else to do."

LaMark stood up and then offered his hand toward Crowe's uninjured fingers. He raised him to his feet. "Come in," he said. "I have a few minutes."

Crowe sat in the living room after accepting an offer of coffee. He could hear LaMark taking a cup from the cupboard. Looking around, he found a modestly decorated living room, but in the corner were both a piano and a harp. He stared, imagining their weight.

"My wife and I play," LaMark said, walking into the living room. He set the cup on the coffee table. "A couple that plays together and all that."

Crowe picked up his drink.

"Well, there you go," said LaMark. "Got that hand back to work already."

His fingers still tingled their complaints, but he could hold and drink from the cup. The heat in the handle felt good against his skin. "I'll be fine."

LaMark took his seat, sipping from his cup. "What did you need to talk about so badly that you were willing to get your fingers chopped off for it?" He smiled.

He wasn't sure how long he had or how long LaMark would listen and so unloaded everything he could like it was a race.

LaMark put up his hands in surrender. "I can't keep up. You're saying this building is ready to collapse at any moment?" He shook his head. "That doesn't seem very plausible."

"Plausible or not, it's true."

LaMark set his coffee down, crossed his arms, and sat back in his seat. "Do you have any kind of proof?"

Much of the proof had disappeared with Crowe's satchel. "How about Operation Epoxy?"

LaMark furrowed his eyebrows. "What about it?"

"Okay," Crowe said, "if you go by the Board's explanations, the cracks in the lower walls are perfectly natural...something that happens in a building this size as it settles. If that's the case, why do anything about them?"

"Just leave unsightly cracks in the wall?"

Crowe shook his head. "I have a five-foot-long crack in my apartment. It's filled with epoxy. It's no less unsightly."

LaMark looked down and brushed something from his shirt. Crowe imagined that he might as well be the crumbs that were knocked to the floor.

"What about the exoskeleton or Operation Steel?"

LaMark smiled. "You're telling me that the exoskeleton and the steel pilings are proof that the Board doesn't care about the problem?"

Crowe pointed at him. "Sir, you just used the word yourself. 'Problem.' So we are both in agreement that the building has a problem?"

He shook his head. "No, I don't think we're in agreement on that at all. There's a problem that you exaggerate into an irrevocable tragedy waiting to happen. You're fueled by conspiracy theories and fear-mongering."

Crowe held his head between his hands. Then he stopped. It wasn't a good look. He needed to remain calm. He looked up and tried to smile.

"I'll admit that the Board has been negligent of the needs of those on the lower floors," LaMark continued. "That's why I ran for a position... and, I'm making a difference."

"Yes," Crowe said, "I know… LaLights." He shook his head. "We'll have well-lit graves."

LaMark set his hands on his knees and then pushed himself to stand resolutely.

"I'm sorry," Crowe said.

"Regardless, I think this conversation has come to its end." He held out his hand, and Crowe handed him his nearly full cup. "I'm not sure if you've heard, but we're in the middle of a bit of a labor situation. I'm trying to study the numbers there to see if the other guilds have a point. And, speaking of numbers, as a board member, I am privy to the calculations. I've seen the numbers from the Refuse and Outbound Bays as compared to the Receiving Bay. Do you know there is more weight leaving this building every day than coming in?"

Crowe stood up too. "Those numbers are fudged."

LaMark's impatient smile flattened against his teeth. "And I suppose you have proof of this?"

"I've seen it. It's true," Crowe said. "As true as all the issues on the lower floors that Burke tells you aren't issues."

LaMark's eyebrows arched up his forehead. "Well, as I mentioned, I only had a few minutes, and I've given you more time than that."

He gestured toward the door.

Crowe took a few steps but then turned around. "Why did you come to Leo's funeral?"

LaMark stood for a moment, thinking. "I caught wind of it. I thought I should go. My father died alone. I guess I've never quite forgiven myself for not being there."

Crowe touched his heart. “My condolences.”

“It was a long time ago.” He put his hand on Crowe’s shoulder and with a gentle push started him again toward the door. “You gave a powerful eulogy considering you didn’t know the man very well. I think if you redirect your energies, you could make a difference for those living on the lower floors. I do admire your tenacity if not your message.” He opened the door to his apartment and, with another gentle push, moved Crowe out into the hallway. “I don’t want to sound too harsh, but I also don’t want you to forget my seriousness when I say that I don’t want you to ever come here again. This is my home.” He shrugged his palms. “And I’m sorry about your hand.”

Crowe nodded. “It’s okay. Thank you for your time.”

Without a parting word, LaMark closed the door.

Crowe dragged his feet down the hall, feeling as though he’d truly ruined the one opportunity he had to convince LaMark. Why hadn’t he brought some kind of proof? And, where the hell was Dagmar? And then a gentler part of him thought—where is she, indeed? Frustrated or not, he missed her. He’d woken the last few nights hoping it was the sound of her key in his door that had stirred him. Instead, it was almost always the super and his wife bickering… or sometimes making love.

Glancing down, he noticed a piece of paper sticking out from under a tenant’s door. Was someone else distributing literature? He crouched and then pulled the flier out. He was surprised to see a picture of a stern-looking Mrs. Montgomery. Above her picture were the words, Bring Them to Heel. Reading, he put it together that her campaign was going to center around the labor agitation taking place in the building. As a board member, she would not be bullied by the demands of workers who she claimed were already well compensated. On a whim, her flier argued, they could not decide when they should be paid more to work less. Their demands threatened the very stability and comfort of life in the building that they had all come to love. The flier ended on the note that, without offering any discussion during the meeting, Fairchild, her opponent, had voted yes to the new Delivery Guild Compensation Package.

Crouching there, reading it for the third time, he guessed that she must have been working with a campaign manager. Someone was helping her craft a message that would land her on the Board. It was no wonder they were sliding these fliers under doors and not posting them around the building. With a slogan like Bring Them to Heel she'd lose votes on some of the middle-lower floors, not to mention the bottom-most. It was a good ruse… if it was a ruse. He wasn't sure what he really knew anymore or who he could trust. Dagmar had left his bed only to go AWOL. LaMark was out of touch when it came to the most crucial issues regarding the building. Maybe Mrs. Montgomery, given time to reflect and under the influence of her son, had changed her mind about what she could truly accomplish on the Board. Maybe her apartment was full of furniture again. His head swam in a haze of fog and mist.

Down the hall, the guest elevator dinged its arrival. Two security guards stepped off the lift and looked directly at him. Their expressions said he was who they'd been hoping to find. Some 300 feet away, they bolted in his direction. On instinct, he ran, letting Mrs. Montgomery's flier loose from his fingers and fluttering to the floor. Reaching it, he mashed his sweating palm into the freight elevator's call button. The men were cutting the distance quickly.

"Stay right there!"

"Shit," Crowe hissed, dashing for the fire door. In the stairwell, he slammed his body into the security gates and took the stairs two at a time, grabbing at railings, and careening off walls. He could hear them pounding behind and gaining on him. Had LaMark called them after he left? His lungs burned. His legs simmered with growing exhaustion. The floor numbers flashed by on the fire doors: 39, 38, 37… And behind him, the sounds of hammering feet getting louder and louder. With six steps left to each flight, he began leaping down to the next landing, suspecting that his pursuers were doing the same. He gulped breaths. Were they gaining? Were they falling behind? The echo chamber of the stairwell reverberating with the piston rhythm of their feet against metal and concrete gave nothing away. He could imagine their hands reaching out for him, their fingertips inches away from his tie flapping over his shoulder like a tail.

Periodically, the voice of a dispatcher came echoing from one of the security guard's shoulder radios. "Susp… 84th floor… appr…ded." He couldn't discern the words but knew that the ghostly static-filled voice was getting closer to him, which meant the guards were getting closer too.

The fire door for the 21st floor flashed by. An idea came to him. Reaching the 20th floor, he pushed open the fire door, closed it as quickly as he could, and sprinted with what he had left down the hallway. He didn't look back. Didn't want to know.

The air in his chest felt cold, and he coughed up a mouthful of phlegm—the resin lining his lungs breaking free from the exertion, some vile residue from all the years of breathing the air of the lower floors. With nowhere to spit, he swallowed it into his empty stomach.

He found the double doors he was looking for: PS 20. He ran past an empty reception desk, past partition walls dividing the large space up into separate rooms. There were last names on plastic signs on the doorways to each makeshift room.

Then he saw it: Simmons.

He stopped right outside the doorway, bent over, catching his breath. He peered back over the distance he'd come from. They weren't behind him.

Not yet.

Then what he was doing occurred to him. Pursued by security guards, he ran into a public school? What was he even thinking? He was going to hide among children, make them witness his being tackled, subdued—or worse put them in danger. He was risking getting Sarah involved, a woman he barely knew. The guards would want to know why he went to her. No, he thought. I can't. He looked back in the direction from where he'd come. Still nobody. No commotion at all. He could leave… had to leave.

"What are you doing?"

He looked up at Sarah Simmons. Behind her, through the doorway, her class was seated at desks, their heads bent to some worksheet.

He panted. "I thought… I… I thought you could use… a guest… a guest speaker. Study skills." He tried to smile.

She looked him over with concern. Her eyes were too kind for him to lie.

"No… Someone's after me. It's… it's… I can go. I'm just going to g—"

She put her hand on his shoulder and guided him into the room where he wedged himself into an empty desk near the back. "Get your breath," she said. She walked to the front of the room.

A handful of the students stole glances over their shoulders and, a few that he tutored, offered smiles and jerky little waves with their hands, even as their puzzled eyes worried about him.

He forced smiles and waved back.

"Your eyes should only be on your quizzes," Mrs. Simmons said. Her voice was different, stern—one used for keeping order. She came back and set a box of tissue on Crowe's desk. "You're sweaty," she said, smiling. After glancing outside of her room, she returned to the front, never once looking at her desk, but instead surveying the students.

Crowe pulled tissues from the box. He mopped his forehead, his face, his neck. The whole time his eyes were on the doorway, but nobody came through. "I lost them," he whispered to himself, stifling a chilled cough that would plague him for the next hour.

When the students finished their quizzes, Mrs. Simmons collected them. She made no mention of their visitor and only scolded, "never you mind," when they looked back at him. On her screen, she projected images, timelines, and dates covering a period of more recent history known as the Ozone Precaution. Crowe observed her and the way her heart had clearly been called to the profession. She moved seamlessly from lecture, to having them discuss in groups, to having a larger discussion with the entire group. She took them seriously and treated them with respect and, in turn, they offered the same to her. It was something that the worst teachers missed. Crowe had had plenty of them through his schooling. Phone it in or betray your apathy for the task at hand and you were finished as far as the students were concerned. Students only needed to know that you had a passion for the subject and a desire for them to learn it. It was never about discipline or order. With the right environment, those came naturally. It was a combination of expertise, humility, an excitement for the material, reverence for the learned and the learners, a varied approach, and genuine acknowledgment of their successes and their missteps. She had it all, and he watched her for hours as though she were a magician.

With pride, he observed Luke and Tim participating. They'd offer something to the discussion, Mrs. Simmons would praise them and, despite her warnings, they'd glance back at Crowe. He offered them quick approval in the gesture of a raised thumb, but with a spin of his finger they'd turned their attention back to the front. It wasn't lost on him that Mrs. Simmons was aware, and he offered her an apologetic shrug if they made eye contact. She smiled in return to accept his apology.

With only 45 minutes left in the school day, Mrs. Simmons finally invited Crowe to the front of the room. Before then, at least one of the school's administrators had looked into the room and had given him a confused stare. Mrs. Simmons had noticed, and when she did invite him to the front of the room, she introduced him as a guest speaker on study skills.

"We have that exam coming up when we meet again next week," she said. "It covers the last three chapters, and with that, Mr. Crowe here is going to help you with strategies for synthesizing all of that information."

She'd put him on the spot. Regardless, he quickly fell back on the same strategies he'd been using in his group tutoring sessions. By the time another administrator looked in the room, Crowe was in full swing and seemed as legitimate as any other guest speaker. The administrator stood in the doorway for a time and eventually nodded his head in approval before leaving.

When the class ended, a few of Crowe's students talked with him, but only briefly, clearly eager to be free of the schoolroom. Mrs. Simmons gathered up her materials and grading books. They walked out together, saying nothing. Aside from some lingering kids, the hallway was empty. Walking about 500 feet, she stopped in front of an apartment door.

"This is me," she said.

He nodded. "Thank you for—"

"I think you should come in for a bit," she said, turning her key in the lock. "If they saw you going into the school, they probably know when school is out. They might be waiting for you." She opened the door and gestured him in.

The one-bedroom apartment was sparsely furnished with no decorations or knick-knacks. Even the walls were bare of pictures. She had a futon sofa with a coffee table in front of it. On the table sat a single book: Once, They Had Pets: a History of Domesticated Animals.

"Please sit down," she said. When she returned from the kitchen, she set down a bottle of Just Like Water for each of them.

Opening the container, he recalled the water in Mrs. Montgomery's apartment. He shook his head. Just Like Water was only like water in appearance. It ran slowly and thick down the throat, like syrup—like swallowing a greased length of rope. Even if left in refrigeration for days, it never cooled below lukewarm. Still, it quenched thirst and didn't taste of rusted metals. He thought of the marketing copy he'd written for JLW. "Doesn't taste of rusted metals," might have been the most positive and accurate thing he could have written about it had he been allowed to be honest. It wasn't honesty but advertising that made JLW the most popular water substitute, far outselling Water Now and Water You Waiting For.

"So, who was chasing you?"

He told her about going to talk to LaMark and then what happened in the hallway afterward.

"I don't know, they just seemed intent. Usually, the security guards will chase you off the floor, and they're satisfied. These guys followed me down thirty flights of stairs." He apologized. "I shouldn't have come to the school, but I guess I was a little spooked." He pointed to the fading bruises on his face. "I had visitors the other night. They were sending a message." He looked into her eyes. "I swear, I wouldn't have gone near the school if I thought it was anybody besides guards behind me."

"You were beat up?"

He nodded. "There are people who don't care for my activism."

Sarah leaned forward and slid the book from the coffee table into her lap. Opening it, she took out the bookmark. The page she turned to had an old photograph of a woman with an animal sitting next to her on a couch. It looked similar to the wolves he'd seen in the zoo documentary. It still struck him as odd that people had once lived that way.

"Is this you?" she asked, handing him the piece of paper she'd been using as a bookmark. "Did you write this?"

It was a flier: What You Don't Know About the Exoskeleton.

He nodded.

"You're a very good writer." She pointed around her sparsely-decorated apartment. "You're a very convincing writer… as you can see." She took the paper from him, set it back in her book, and then set the volume back on the table.

"This is… I mean, living like this is to reduce the load?" he asked, gesturing toward the apartment. He flipped his palms up sympathetically and then set his hands back on his knees. "I didn't want to ask. I didn't know how much teachers make."

She laughed. "No, I could have more than this. I'm just trying to make a difference, you know? I teach history, and you won't find one book in my apartment besides the few I have checked out from the library." She put her hands to her cheeks and exhaled. "It wasn't easy, but I brought my collection to the Refuse Ramp about six months ago."

He raised his eyebrows. "That's commitment."

She touched the bruise under his left eye and then retracted her hand. "I think *this* is commitment."

He smiled. "Well, you might be the only person who read my material and did something." He thought of Mrs. Montgomery. "Well, maybe you're among a handful. I'm just not sure that's worth the beating I took." He thought back to the sizzling backhands and shuddered.

She said if history had taught her anything, it was that it can take a long time for people to change, but they do change. "History is the study of how we changed. Just keep getting your message out. Give it time. It's not like I read your first pamphlet and immediately started living lighter."

"Isn't some of history about how we failed to change?"

She nodded. "That too. But that usually still ends with some kind of change."

He thought of Dagmar. "I'm just not sure we have a lot of time for the change to happen."

"You think something could happen soon?"

He told her that the language in his literature was watered down.

"It's a fine line. It has to be palatable. People won't read anything that sounds over the top. But, if I wrote what I think needs to be written, with the right urgency, it would just fuel the conspiracy theory talk. And any thinking person, like yourself, would just weep."

He set his head back on the futon's cushion. "I don't know. I don't even know what I don't know." Sighing, he turned toward her. "I don't want to talk about the building right now if that's okay. Aside from spending time in your class and now with you, it's been a pretty bad day. I should head home."

She put her hand on his wrist. "I don't think you should just yet." She took her hand away. "Let me make you dinner." She laughed. "It's the least I can do considering the free seminar you gave my students today."

"I didn't have breakfast or lunch." He nodded. "I could eat, Mrs. Simmons."

She smiled. "Please, call me Sarah."

In the kitchen, she rehydrated lasagna, and corn, and put out bread with margarine. Taking it from a top shelf, she poured a box of powdered wine into a carafe mixed with JLW and rusty tap water and stirred it until it became merlot. They sat at her small kitchen table. Sarah held a tightly meshed strainer over his glass while pouring from the carafe.

"Little less chewy this way," she said

The conversation turned quickly to their lives. Sarah was living on the same floor she'd grown up on, teaching at the same school she'd attended. Both of her parents had been teachers at the school. They still lived on 20 as well. Their apartment was only several hundred feet from hers. Dedicating her life to teaching, she'd never tried to meet anyone.

"Most of the men I meet talk about wanting children. The way they talked, it seemed like they assumed I would eventually get married, quit my job, and raise children at home. For me, it's always been enough to devote myself to the children in my classes."

He nodded. "Me? I fell into tutoring out of necessity, but sometimes I'll be in the middle of it, and it will hit me that I'm doing something I was born to do."

She raised her glass to him. "As I said, you are good."

They touched their glasses together and each took a sip. He felt a calm looking into her eyes. There was depth and caring there.

He told her about marketing for JLW and how he had lived on the 26th floor for a time.

"I went to college for acting, but ended up in marketing."

He mentioned how the stage theaters below the 70th floor had largely vanished and with that any real chance of him acting.

"The work for JLW never meant anything to me, but I was good at it. It gave me a life and things I was supposed to want, but at some point, I realized I never really wanted those things to begin with."

He told her about his parents. "My father worked on the maintenance crew. He used to grumble about shortcuts they were taking, shortsighted decisions the Board was making. At the time, I wrote him off as a hardworking, but bitter, hyperbolic man. I felt it was an unfortunate symptom of being uneducated. The truth is, one becomes blind to wisdom because you doubt the intelligence of the source. Turns out he *was* onto something."

She reached across the table and squeezed his hand. "It must have been difficult to lose your parents when you were so young."

He squeezed her hand back and the warmth in her palm washed into his.

"It was a turning point, I know that much. Still, there's a degree of acting to what I do. Standing at peoples' doors or tutoring… there's performance involved as much as anything."

"That's true… same with teaching."

They stood side by side at her sink. She handed him dripping plates or silverware, and he dried them.

Flexing his wounded, reddened hand in the air in front of him, he told her about his visit to LaMark.

"It sounds like you missed your calling as a door-to-door salesman. That's quite a technique to keep the sales pitch going over crushed fingers," she said, laughing.

"Hey," he said, smiling himself.

Putting away the casserole pan, which was the last of the dishes, he closed the cupboard. She stood for a moment staring into the frosted window of her kitchen. The gray beyond the glass was ever-present.

"It sometimes feels like we haven't learned anything… from the past," she said.

Without turning on any lights, they sat for some time on the futon in the darkness of the living room. His hand found hers and they laced their fingers together. Their honest, human talk was like divination, and he felt it summoning a contentedness in him he hadn't felt in a long time, if ever. In time, their talk drifted back to the fate of the building.

"I don't think people are inherently evil or selfish," she said. "We just seem to have a hard-wired stubbornness for rationalizing our own beliefs and behaviors."

"I have a friend," Crowe started, "who thinks we could have as little as five months. Even if that's exaggerated, it's coming. Honestly, I don't think anyone can do anything about it."

She was quiet for a moment. "I hadn't heard anything that dire," she whispered.

"I believe it is that dire."

They went silent, as though the heaviness they'd talked into the air suppressed the ability for any more words.

Crowe stood up. "I think I should be going."

She told him she didn't think he should. "Just to be safe."

She stood then and started to convert the futon into a bed.

He didn't argue. He didn't want to go back to his empty apartment. She brought him a sheet and while she left to find a blanket, he undressed and climbed into the cool cocoon of her linen. She draped the blanket over him when she returned, then left without a word back into her bedroom.

He waited, but she didn't come back. He shook his head. He'd been too morose. What did he know? Would it be five months? Could it be a year? Maybe the building would never come down. Maybe all of ACT's funereal predictions were the stuff of paranoia and gloom that others always said they were. And here he'd ruined a good evening with his words. Again. As always. Now he lay on her couch, a guest of pity.

I can't stay here, he thought and made to throw the bed-covers off of himself when Sarah emerged again into the living room. She was wearing a white nightgown, looking like a ghost in the low light.

"May I lie with you?"

He stared at her for a moment. "I may be with someone."

She paused in her approach. "What?"

He put his head back on the pillow and looked up into the darkness of the ceiling.

"I don't know… there's another woman. It could be there's nothing there. I just wanted you to know."

She folded back the blanket and sheet and climbed in with him. "I don't want to sleep alone. I don't think I've ever been more afraid in my life."

He scooted closer to her and pressed the warmth of his chest against the heat of her back. She reached for his arm and draped it over her. Their fingers braided again and nestled between her breasts. The night pressed heavy against the window, and they lay together, as though buoyed by a raft, on that darkling plain.

In the morning, he was alone. In the middle of the night had she thought better of it and retreated to her bed?

Answering his thought, she came out of the bedroom pulling a shoe onto her foot. She wore the same green dress she'd worn when they'd first met.

"I have school in ten minutes," she said.

He lay watching her… the bend of her calves as she worked at the second shoe.

"There was an apartment invasion yesterday morning on the 107th floor," she said, standing from her task.

"What?"

She nodded. "I just came off of a video call with my mom. The guy was dressed like he was from Delivery. When the husband opened the door, he pushed his way in and bludgeoned them both to death." She explained that the husband's body was found in the kitchen, and the wife's in the bedroom. "They were in their seventies. The wife locked the bedroom door, but I guess the guy came right through it."

Crowe's mind raced with thoughts of the night on the Receiving Bay. What did he know about the people Dagmar had recruited? Had one of them held onto the delivery uniform? Would they go that far? To what end?

"Maybe that's why the guards chased you."

Crowe sat bolt upright. "Do they… do you think they think I…?"

She shook her head. "No, they caught him on the 84th floor. Some guy from the 52nd. An accountant. He'd been dating their granddaughter. The grandparents didn't approve, so she broke things off with him."

"So he killed them?"

She nodded. "Sounds like it." She crossed her arms. "Love can make people crazy."

"And he was…?"

She nodded. "Banished."

Banished from the building. A death sentence. Crowe sat numb for a moment trying to process everything she'd just told him. Ready to leave, she stepped over to the futon, hovering over him. He looked up into her green, inviting eyes.

"I would like to see you again, Harvey, but I think you should figure out your other situation before we do."

"I will," he said.

She opened the door. "Goodbye. Thanks for staying with me."

"Thank you for—"

She closed the door.

He lay for a moment in the growing melancholy that he knew leaving her apartment would mean. Waking once in the night, he found himself still enveloped in her embrace. In that moment, he had hoped for the night to just keep going… for the light to never come to the window. In time, he rose, dressed slowly, and folded the sheet and blanket. The mechanics of the futon eluded him for a moment, but he was able to finally get it back in the shape of a couch.

Outside, the 20th floor hallway was quiet save for a few straggling children running past him toward the school. The stairwell was empty too. Opening the fire door to his floor, he half-expected someone from Security to be waiting for him. There was nobody. They'd caught the guy, he told himself. Why would they still be after me?

Outside his door sat a package too big for the delivery box. He guessed it had just recently arrived otherwise it would have been stolen. He opened his door and hefted the weight of the box onto his kitchen table. As he ran a knife's edge across the packing tape, he remembered what he'd find inside. Lying in his bed, recovering from the assault, he'd ordered them. He opened the flaps of the box to reveal two jimmy-resistant deadbolts, a barrel bolt, two chain locks, an adjustable security bar, a door frame and hinge reinforcements, a swing bar door guard, and a brass door brace. Lying in the residual simmering of his pain, he'd added each to his virtual shopping cart, though he knew he couldn't afford them.

His mind did the math: 20 to 25 pounds. And for what? A false sense of security. If anyone wanted to hurt him, it would happen regardless of how many locks he purchased. He closed the flaps and retrieved a roll of packing tape from his utility drawer. Then he sealed the box. He would bring it to the Outgoing Bay later that day.

He fell into his bed but felt rested. What a night's sleep he'd had. His contentment didn't last for long.

"I want only for you to die, Sam. Do you hear me?"

"Trust me, it would be sweet relief, you brooding, bloated bitch!"

CHAPTER 8

The top of Crowe's kitchen table was covered in papers and photographs that he'd salvaged from different places in his apartment. He sorted through them, placing them into different file folders. Some were past reports from the Board. Others came from varied, if questionable, sources. Whatever evidence he had of the truth of the situation was thin and circumspect. He slapped a file shut.

"It's not enough," he said aloud.

Examining it, the crack in his kitchen wall had extended two more inches. He touched his fingertip into the building's wound, one of many. What had once been water, sand, and gravel bound together by limestone and clay was becoming, not its original components, but some manmade emptiness and dust. What it could once hold up was becoming what it would soon not endure.

Events had moved swiftly over the last three weeks. The building had held its most recent elections. Burke had tried to cancel them, stating that the Board was facing unprecedented challenges that couldn't possibly be understood by new board members. The vote for such a cancelation had turned against him since there was too much grumbling from the upper floor tenants. Nobody on the Board wanted to risk their future seat by voting on something that looked like suppression. Most were running uncontested, so it didn't matter to them anyway. For the first time, Director Fairsmith had spoken at length during the discussion portion of the motion:

"More than any time before, this board needs the constancy of long-time members. A vote for new members now may very well undermine the fabric of the Board and this building."

Most looked down into their laps as he spoke or smiled at him sympathetically. His seat was a sacrifice they were willing to make.

The Board had already taken a calculated risk. Only two weeks before, after a two-day work reduction by the Maintenance Guild, the Board had voted in favor of giving the maintenance personnel a raise. Struggling against Mrs. Montgomery's campaign's growing popularity, Fairsmith was the only director to vote against the maintenance raise. Instead of coming across as a reasoned vote, most saw it as desperation on his part. The raise was not a board decision that met with much approval from tenants on the upper floors. The vote had been followed by a decision to increase co-op fees to cover the costs. It was rumored that the Security Guild had wanted to join with maintenance on a work reduction demonstration, but after the apartment invasion and subsequent murders, they felt it wasn't the right time.

Industrialists in the building quietly floated their long-time idea that security could easily be handled by robotic guards and increased surveillance. The Board had long argued that residents wouldn't feel comfortable with cameras in the hallways—too much of a privacy invasion.

Crowe guessed that in her astute, cynical wisdom, Dagmar would have said, "Of course not. It would be too easy to monitor the delivery infractions if there were cameras in the hallways."

Most in the building weren't comfortable with the idea, even though after the initial investment, the robotic guards would be less expensive than human personnel over the long term. In the past, the manufacturers had often ended their presentations to the Board with this final statement: "Robots don't call in sick and can't be bribed." This reinvigorated campaign for mechanized security largely kept the Security Guild neutered.

Word had leaked on the middle and lower floors about Mrs. Montgomery's campaign slogan to "Bring Them to Heel." Regardless, she won in a landslide against Fairsmith. It confirmed for Crowe that she was likely correct about the Board not even counting the lower floor votes. She was viewed by upper tenants as a necessary stopgap—a break wall against the mounting "proletariat unrest" that was stirring through the building. The guilds, all with new presidents since the elections, were meeting nightly to reevaluate the conditions of their contracts. In a month, they would begin their yearly negotiations with the Board. Where past negotiations had gone smoothly with the begrudging guild members having the need for cuts or pay freezes explained to them, the upcoming negotiations were anticipated to be rancorous.

Crowe wasn't certain if it was because of his visit to his apartment, but LaMark had motioned that they consider an annual Spring Cleaning 100 Day. The 100 was to stand for 100 tons of reduced load. He couched it as a precautious effort to take any unnecessary pressure off of the exoskeleton and steel pilings. Even the chairman spoke in favor of LaMark's motion.

"More than anything," Burke said, "we don't want unforeseen conditions slowing down the construction of what will be three more floors of beautiful penthouse apartments." During a recent board meeting, one of the Board's architects had guardedly raised doubts about the building's ability to handle more floors. "It is a move that could have structural ramifications in the decades ahead," he admitted. The architect was let go the next day.

In his own continued use of discussion time, LaMark reiterated that his original proposal was in the name of the building's general health, and not necessarily to ensure that new floors would be added. "The addition of new floors and the need for a voluntary reduction in load are two separate issues. I do, however, appreciate the chairman's support of the motion." The motion did pass, but Crowe's heart had sunk when he saw that Mrs. Montgomery had voted against it.

What she'd voted against had turned out to be a sham. A few days after the vote, they held the building's first Spring Cleaning 100 Day. They had a scale at the Refuse Ramp and trucks scheduled to make regular pickups on the hour for five hours. Crowe heard from people in Delivery that only one truck had been filled three-quarters of the way. Then, that same truck later came up the Receiving Ramp, where delivery people had a list of specific items that were to be returned to apartments. Some tenants, as it turned out, had participated as a show, while others witnessing the limited participation of others had changed their minds. And so, when the lone truck finally departed, it had taken with it about 15 tons of load.

In its next meeting, Chairman Burke opened with a report on the success of Spring Cleaning 100, noting that they fell just shy of their goal, according to the scale in the Refuse Bay. "Next year will be even more successful," Burke concluded. "We are doing what we need to do without intruding on people's comfort."

Crowe looked again through the papers on his table. He had the printout from the delivery scale to show how little weight had actually left during the so-called Spring Cleaning. It wasn't enough, though. All the evidence he had wasn't enough. "'Next year'," he mumbled, mocking Burke's voice. "What next year?"

His mind went to Dagmar, as it always did. He stood up from the table and paced the tiny space of his kitchen. Opening the drawer, he took out a switchblade. When he'd seen someone from ACT in the hallway just days ago, he mentioned that he still had their weapons. That they should come to get them. None did. He pressed the button and the handle flicked out its silvery tongue. His reflection in the steel showed bags under his eyes, chapped lips, and sallow skin. He struggled to try to find a way to retract it, and then finally set it clanking back to the drawer with the blade still exposed.

He'd heard nothing from Dagmar. Nobody had. Nobody even knew where she lived or where to start looking for her. She seemed a spirit—something invoked more than corporeal—something that appeared when one's mind was most turned to kicking in the teeth of those who wouldn't listen. "Burke. I hate him," Crowe might think. "Me too," she'd say and there she would be standing behind him, making barbwire look as though it should be worn as jewelry. At least that's how she appeared to him in his dreams.

He'd never been to her apartment. He figured her secrecy was something she'd done for her protection, maybe knowing how serious the fight might get. It made him wonder if his openness was a misstep on his part. He'd believed honesty would aid the cause and so was generous with his phone number, his name. Recently however, sounds in the hallways woke him throughout the night, when before he'd sleep easily through them. He regretted sending back the locks and extra door security.

He had nightmares that replayed the events of his assault. The dreams started with his door being kicked in as though it was made of toothpicks. He'd wake shivering in his drenched sheets, his heart clamoring for release from his chest. Then, too, he knew that if he'd installed the locks, he might never see Dagmar again appearing in his bedroom doorway full of her indifferent lust.

To calm himself after the nightmares, he would remember his night with Sarah Simmons. He could feel his fingers entwined in hers. From her too, he'd heard nothing in the weeks since they had lain together on her futon. His urge to see her, to be with her again, was a physical ache. And still, his feelings and thoughts for Dagmar lingered, a craving to his unhealthy addiction. He needed to know at the very least that she was okay… still alive.

The building had changed since the apartment invasion on the upper floors. Following Operation Keep Them Safe, anyone living on the lower floors was restricted from movement above the 25th floor, even though the investigation revealed that the assailant had been from a much higher floor. Students who lived between the 25th and 29th floors were crammed into classrooms in the 20PS. The Security Guild had doubled the shifts of their guards without additional pay. Even the delivery personnel couldn't help Crowe in his attempts to get to the higher floors. Now, a security guard attendant acted as a sentry in every elevator in the building, including the freight elevator.

It's boiling over, Crowe thought. The tensions in the building were an aneurysm waiting to explode, and yet nobody was talking about the threat that faced all of them. He stalked his papers… his evidence. How would all his calculations resonate in an environment of labor unrest, fears of murderous break-ins, and the alleged success of the Spring Cleaning?

His message? His warnings? Was it all just white noise, a niggling insect buzzing around the ear—easily swatted away and smashed against the cracking walls?

He set his hands on all of it—all the papers, the words, and the numbers—and swept them to the floor, a brief chaos and cacophony of flapping pages, and then silence. It was after midnight. There was nothing for it, he decided, except to go to bed.

Later, he woke, as he often had… to the echo of it in his memory—the sound of the key hitting the lock, the door whispering open, of her feet padding down the hallway toward his bedroom. The shish and zip sounds of her stripping off clothing to be, and yet not to be, with him. But she was never there. He looked up into the ceiling and sighed forlornly.

"Why so sad?"

He sat up. She was leaning against the doorway as she always had before. Then too there was something different about the silhouette. Her arm…it was in a sling?

"Dagmar? Is that you?"

"Still sharp as ever, eh Crowe?"

Even bolstered by sarcasm her voice was raspy and exhausted. She stepped further into the room, disappearing into the darkness.

"The other shoe is dropping."

Crowe fumbled for the switch on his lamp.

"Don't! I don't want you to see me like this."

He heard her set something on the floor.

"What happened to you?" he asked. "Where have you been?"

He heard her back sliding against the wall, lowering herself to the floor. Soft, agonized moans accompanied her effort.

"Dagmar?"

"Jeez. Give me a second."

He listened as she adjusted herself—the small, closed-mouth noises in her throat playing the notes to her dirge of pain.

"I'm okay. This is better." Her breaths were labored. "I just needed some time to think… sorry that I've been out of contact."

He sat for a moment in the silence.

"What were you thinking about?"

"Us, Crowe. I was thinking about us. I mean, maybe we should get married. I'm ready to settle down… maybe have a baby. A little girl. What do you think of the name Jessica?" She laughed, but the strained sound of it turned into coughing. "What the hell do you think I was thinking about?"

"Okay. Okay." He crossed his arms. "I didn't imagine you were thinking about us."

She was quiet again for a time, collecting the energy to speak. "I have a plan. I think it's our only shot, but I need your help fleshing it out." She told him she agreed with him about LaMark and Peoples, that they could be allies.

"I don't know about that Montgomery, though. I mean, 'Bring Them to Heel?'"

He told her he thought it was just a campaign strategy. "It worked too. Fairsmith is gone."

She made another muted sound in her throat, registering the pain somewhere in her body.

"I told you I didn't trust her. I still don't."

"I'm not sure if I do anymore either. I guess I'm not sure of anything."

"Well, I have proof. Everything is in this bag. Facts. Stuff I've had. New stuff. You won't believe some of it."

"I'm more worried about other people not believing it," he said.

She groaned.

"Are you okay?"

She told him that she likely had some broken ribs. "It hurts to talk." She laughed painfully. "Ironic, isn't it… when I actually want to use words instead of my fists?"

He pushed the blankets off and sat on the edge of the bed. "Tell me, what happened?"

"Don't come over here."

"I'm not… just, what happened?"

She was quiet for a long time.

"I had some visitors too… like yours. In a stairwell. If somebody hadn't come in there, I think they would have killed me." She took in a quavering breath. "I think someone's terrified. And desperate. Maybe Burke. Whatever we're going to do needs to happen now… or we might not be here to do it."

"Okay," he said, "what's your plan then?"

"Can I bunk in with you?"

He stood up. "Of course."

"Jesus, you're not getting any, Crowe. I just need to lie down."

"I didn't think—"

She laughed and it had some of the strength of her laughter he'd heard in the past. "I want you to go to the kitchen. I'll call you when I'm ready."

He told her he could help her.

"I know, but I don't want help. Just go."

He made his way out of the room, catching a glance of her—a balled-up darkness, darker than the darkness that surrounded her.

He paced between the cupboard and the wall. Then, thinking of it, he took one of his kitchen chairs and jammed it under the doorknob of the front door as a brace.

"Okay," she called, her voice reedy and thin.

He returned to the bedroom. The form of her was lying in the spot farthest from the wall. He crawled in doing his best not to disturb her. He lay facing the back of her head.

"You can't stay here, Crowe. From what I know, this has to be your last night here."

"Well, I—"

"Go to your teacher, the Simmons woman. Hide there."

He paused a moment in a pang of sudden guilt. "You know about her?"

"Yes, and I don't care. We were never going to be anything. I'm not built that way, or if I ever was it has been broken out of me." She coughed. "Oh…"

He touched her shoulder. "I think you should go to the infirmary."

She let him keep his hand on her bare skin.

"Negative. Now, just listen. I need some help with aspects of the plan."

She began, in almost a whisper, to explain her plan to him. Then, she dozed off with his hand still on her shoulder. He stayed awake as long as he could, feeling closer to her than he ever had before, but closeness with the fondness of friendship in it. He worked over the holes in her plan and came up with additional strategies that might work. When he woke in the morning, he wasn't surprised to find her gone. Her bag sat on the floor—a beacon. He pulled it over to the edge of the bed and began to sift through it.

It was everything they needed… or at least had to be.

CHAPTER 9

They lay in Sarah's bed with the gray dawn slowly fading in through the window's frosted glass. She had her arm draped over his chest.

"I'm glad you're here," she said.

"I'm glad you took me in."

He pulled her hand up to his mouth and kissed the back of it.

"I guess this is what it feels like to be part of a revolution."

She took her arm from his chest and put both of her hands behind her head on the pillow. "I've taught so many different eras of our history, and I always wondered about those with the bravery to say, 'This is enough. We need to do something.'."

"There's always a risk," he said. "You don't have to help if you're afraid."

She rolled toward him. "The fear I have for the future if we do nothing far outweighs any fear I have about you being here with me."

He nodded. "This might be the only way to have a future."

She traced her finger along one of his ribs. "I can't believe what you showed me."

He smiled sympathetically. "You can't? You're a student of history. There's the in-group and the out-group, and more often than not that comes down to the haves and the have nots."

She rolled to her back again. "Not always… there's race. There's religion. Lots of ugliness involved there."

"Lots of haves and have-nots in all that mess, too."

"True. It's just difficult to process when it's made so plain." She rolled her legs and then stood up out of the bed. "I need to get ready for work."

Watching her walk naked across the room, Crowe had a hard time swallowing.

"You're a vision," he said.

She threaded her arms through the loops of her bra and began working at the hooks.

"That might be overstating it, but I don't mind hearing it."

"I'll be here when you get back."

She smiled at him. "I don't mind hearing that either."

Crowe spent the morning and the early afternoon pacing her apartment. He tried to eat, having prepared something rehydrated, but found that he didn't have an appetite. Several times his mind went to Dagmar and he weighed the emotions he felt. It wasn't longing exactly, more of a concern. In bed next to her the few times that he was, he could feel the chill coming off of her body. She'd shiver, and as quietly as he could, he'd pull the blankets up around her restless movements. In time, she'd kick and flail them away, as though even in sleep she wanted nothing from anyone. He hoped where ever she was that she was warm. He hoped she was healing.

Around two o'clock in the afternoon, someone knocked on Sarah's door. It resounded through the sparsely furnished space. Sick with adrenaline, he pushed the button to engage her video peephole. Nothing happened.

"Unbelievable," he muttered. Then: "Who's there?"

He expected the gruff voice of someone from Security.

"It's Director LaMark."

Crowe scrambled through the locks and opened the door.

LaMark was holding an envelope. "What is this?"

Crowe recognized his handwriting on it. He had included no return address and had slipped it into someone's outgoing mail on the 22nd floor. Relief washed through him like an elixir.

"You got it," he said.

"Yes, but what is it?"

Crowe offered for him to come in. He double-checked the empty hallway before closing the door behind them. They sat on the futon. Crowe held out his hand, and LaMark handed him the envelope. He opened it and withdrew a piece of paper covered with construction schematics. He laid it on the table in front of them.

"This is a blueprint for a panic room being built on the 110th floor," Crowe said. "One of many."

After the apartment invasion, the Board had held an emergency meeting. People living on the upper floors were terrified. They wanted something to be done. For them, doubling the rounds of the security sweeps on each floor was not enough. The Board voted that, especially in light of the Spring Cleaning success, tenants would be allowed to convert an existing room in their apartment into a panic room.

LaMark picked up the blueprint, looked at it, and then set it down again. He shrugged. “I guess I don’t see what I’m supposed to see. Your note said that this is of life or death.”

Crowe crossed his arms. “The Board voted that the tenants could do this.”

LaMark crossed his arms in return. “Yes. We did.” He cleared his throat. “That poor woman might still be alive if she’d had somewhere safe to run. That animal went through that bedroom door like it was tissue paper.”

Crowe rubbed his fingertips into his forehead. “Do you really believe there are going to be a rash of violent break-ins? It sounded like an isolated incident. The attacker had a grudge against the victims. Tragic, for sure, but not a sign of a crime epidemic.”

LaMark stood up. “People are scared. What would you have us do… nothing? I voted in favor of this, and I’m proud of the vote. Why did you even send—”

“What did you vote on? Do you know the details?”

LaMark pointed at him, his face a flush of anger. “Mr. Crowe, if you’re implying that I just vote arbitrarily without considering the—”

“The panic rooms, then. What were the details?”

Crowe felt a drop of sweat break from under his arm and slide coolly along his ribs.

LaMark shook his head. “You sonuvabitch, what is this? Is this some kind of test? Then I’ll tell you exactly what I voted for.” It was simple enough. Tenants could take an existing interior room and replace one wooden door and doorjamb with steel. "Any additional weight is negligible. And given the sense of peace that—"

Crowe nodded. "Exactly, negligible… if people follow the code. The thing is, many people aren't following the weight codes. In fact, most aren't." He gestured toward the futon. "If you'll sit down for a moment, I can tell you exactly what this drawing means," he said, pointing to the blueprint.

LaMark hesitated, but finally sat down.

"What, then? Show me."

Crowe pulled the blueprint closer to him. "This here calls for the demolition of the existing walls of an interior room. The walls would then be replaced with a concrete wall reinforced on both sides by three-inch-thick steel panels ." He tapped the piece of paper. "Mr. LaMark, we are talking about twenty tons of additional weight per panic room… at least."

LaMark sat stunned for a moment looking at the piece of paper. Then he picked it up and examined it. "Is this legitimate?"

Crowe nodded. "These are the plans for a room that is slated to start tomorrow. We are in contact with an electrician who has wired two such rooms already. Two! There are dozens planned."

LaMark stared at the paper as though it were a biblical prophecy of doom. "Can… can I keep this?"

Crowe reached forward and snatched the blueprint and envelope. "No. It was meant only to inform you."

"A copy then?"

Crowe shook his head.

LaMark crossed his arms. “You can’t expect I am just going to talk about this. I won’t be believed without some kind of proof. What do you want me to say to—”

“I don’t want you to say anything.”

They locked eyes for a moment.

Crowe smiled. “I want you to make a motion at tomorrow night’s meeting that the Board hears from an informed tenant.”

LaMark could only stare. He didn’t blink.

Crowe clapped his hands together and rubbed his palms against each other. “Talk to as many directors as you can before then. Drum up the votes. Lie to them if you have to. Tell them I have positive news to share about ramifications from the Spring Cleaning.”

“That doesn’t seem very ethical.”

Crowe laughed and then abruptly stood. He marched off to the bedroom, dug through his bag of papers, and returned. “Was the Spring Cleaning ethical? That dog and pony show you put on?”

“Now wait a minute. I—”

Crowe handed him the paper.

“Look at that. That’s the printout from the scale that day.” He told him about people having their items redelivered back to their apartments. “Was that ethical? Burke up there reporting, ‘We narrowly missed our goal.’ Off by 85% doesn’t sound like a near miss to me. And he’s using those numbers to sell the idea of adding more floors.”

LaMark looked at the papers, his eyes misting over. “I meant it as a good thing.” He looked up at Crowe. “I looked at some of your literature. I meant—”

"It's worse. I told you the numbers are being fudged. Believe me, Burke has spun the information so many ways it's surprising the weight of his lies alone hasn't brought this place down." Hearing what he'd just said, he followed up with: "and they will."

LaMark absently set the papers on the table. "I've been a fool."

Crowe sat and set his hand on the man's shoulder. "No, you haven't. You've done good things. You've had your heart in a good place. It just needs to go to a bigger place, that's all."

They sat for a moment in silence.

"Why does it have to be you?" LaMark asked. "If you gave me your evidence, I could just as easily present it. I could—"

"It has to be me. You just have to trust me."

LaMark exhaled. "That vote might not go as you want."

"You'll have to make that happen. Whatever you have to do."

"And what if I can't?"

"Then I guess it's over."

They looked at each other.

"Look," Crowe said, "there's a plan. All I'm asking is that you talk to as many other directors as you can. Like I said, lie to them if you have to." He forced a grin. "They're used to it."

LaMark sat for a moment, studying the gray light at the window. His eyes seemed to look into a new distance, as though he were seeing something for the first time. Then, he slapped his hands onto his thighs and pushed himself to stand. "I'm going to get started. I'm going to get you those votes."

"And if you don't, we have a backup plan. I don't want you to feel that this is all on you."

Crowe extended his hand, and in return LaMark offered his firm grip.

Crowe said nothing, only nodded.

"I apologize if I've been obtuse about this. I tend to fixate on my own goals."

Crowe smiled. "I understand."

LaMark gave a weak grin. "It's just hard to believe that we more or less got ourselves—you know, all of us—into this spot."

"Is it that hard to believe? Considering everything that a few people were able to gain from it?"

LaMark thought for a moment. "I guess it isn't," he said, shaking his head.

CHAPTER 10

Crowe stood outside the double doors of the boardroom. He was flanked on either side by three of the largest members of the Delivery Guild. Two security guards stood on either side of the doors, saying nothing.

Crowed leaned forward and with his fingertips pushed one of the doors slightly ajar. The Board was in session approving the minutes from the previous meeting. One of the security guards eyed Crowe, at the same time eyeing the thick delivery men.

Crowe looked at him. "I don't think it's right the flack your guild is taking for what happened in that apartment. That was a freak incident, not a symptom of your guild not doing its job."

The guard tilted his head. "Thanks."

Crowe moved toward a mirror only a few feet away. The delivery workers started to follow. He held up his hand. "I'll be alright."

He examined himself in the glass. Sarah had borrowed one of the suits her father used to wear when he taught. It fit Crowe surprisingly well, although the shoes were too tight on his feet. She'd also given him a haircut. The bruises on his face had largely faded. He nodded. He looked good, or at least as good as he could. He walked back over to the doors.

Burke was in the middle of delivering a report on Operation Living Space.

"... we've worked closely with architects and contractors, and it is with great enthusiasm that I can announce that construction of three new penthouse floors will begin next week. Overall costs match up with the initial budget estimates. Some initial outlay was necessary for longer-lasting hazmat suits purchased from Coldwater Industries, but with that expense comes more speedy construction. Given existing pre-order security deposits from desirous tenants, the project..."

Crowe paced away from the door, shaking his head. They were doing it. Knowing everything they knew, every risk involved, every life at stake, they were going to move forward with the construction project. Greed. Pure greed. He slammed his fist into his other open hand, and then looked down, surprised by the aggression in his seemingly reflexive gesture. One of the guards gave him a look. Calm down, Crowe thought. He slipped back to the doors.

"We have no unfinished business, so on to new business."

"I have something."

Crowe's heartbeat quickened. He set his sweaty palm against the heavy wooden door.

"Director Harris, go ahead."

Crowe sighed. Harris had beaten LaMark out of the gate. Or, had LaMark changed his mind? He began pacing. If they had to go with their backup plan, it would be chaos. He tried his best to push out any negative thoughts. He returned to his position at the doors, not wanting to miss whatever Harris was proposing.

"…light of raises that were granted to the Maintenance and Delivery Guilds, I would like…"

In his peripheral vision, Crowe saw the guards on either side of him lean in closer to the opening between the doors.

"…to make a motion that we establish a Security Appreciation Day next month."

"Jesus Christ," one of the guards muttered. They both leaned back into their original positions.

"Second."

Discussion began. Some spoke to concur with the idea, especially given how the security personnel had been so maligned as of late. One director objected, noting that it might be too soon for such a gesture.

Crowe could only see Burke. He held his gavel like a war hammer, his flinty gaze pivoting around the table.

"Point of information."

Burke turned his head. "Yes, Director Manslett?"

"I would just like to point out that a memorial service is planned for the deceased next month. We should bear that in mind."

"Thank you, Director Manslett." Burke turned his head again, his eyes narrowing in disapproval. "Yes, Director Peoples."

"I would like to make a motion to amend the original motion so that we replace the Appreciation Day with a two percent raise. People can't buy groceries or shoes for their kids with appreciation."

"We can save the editorializing for discussion," Burke said, tapping his gavel against the sound block, "should your motion to amend get a second."

"At least *she* doesn't have her head up her ass," one of the guards said.

Crowe smiled, both at the guard's comment but also hearing LaMark second the motion to amend.

Discussion followed. One director argued that a raise wouldn't be fiscally prudent given the raises that the other guilds had received, not to mention the investment in the new floors that wouldn't be generating revenue for several months. Another pointed out that they would soon be negotiating with the guilds anyway, and perhaps that would be the better suited time for discussing the possibility of a raise. Yet another said that a two percent raise might be preemptive because the Security Guild would surely ask for more than that during negotiations. Finally, someone raised the idea that the appreciation day could be an annual event, which would offer ongoing goodwill, where a raise would diminish in value over time given inflation.

One of the guards looked at the other. "How'd you like to pick out toppings for a pizza with these sonsabitches? They'd likely discuss the merits of mushrooms for half an hour," he said mockingly.

Crowe had to let the door close to stifle his laughter. Recovering, he pressed the door and peeked in again. Peoples' motion to amend the original motion with the two percent raise did not pass. Another motion to amend was offered and seconded, and it involved detailing what exactly the Appreciation Day would include, given the short time involved to make preparations. Someone offered that trying to plan the day on the floor would not be a good use of the Board's time. The amendment was yet amended again to include the wording should the original motion pass, then an ad hoc committee would be formed immediately to begin planning what was feasible for the special day. More amendments were made, and in the end, the Board voted on and approved a new motion to postpone the vote on the original motion to a date that would be more sensitive to the unfortunate incident that had recently occurred. The language included that should the Security Guild garner a raise of higher than one percent in the forthcoming negotiations that there would be no reason to return to the original motion because that would defeat the purpose of having a Security Appreciation Day. If everything fell into place and the original motion passed, at that time selection of an ad hoc Appreciation Day Planning committee would begin.

Burke banged his sound block. "I will set that we will revisit the motion in three months as old business."

"Oh man, now I'm on pins and needles," one of the guards said.

Despite himself, Crowe had to let the door close again to chuckle into the back of his hand. Just as quickly, he put his palm back to the brass plate and made a slight split between the doors. Burke was looking again with the same hint of disdain that he'd shown for Director Peoples.

"Director LaMark?"

Crowe took a deep breath.

"Yes, I'd like to make a motion that an informed tenant be allowed to address the Board."

Burke stared at him. "An informed tenant? I don't understand the motion. In what way is this relevant to new business?"

"He has information that—"

"Mr. Chairman, point of order. Director LaMark has made a motion, and we are moving to discussion prior to the motion being seconded."

"That's true." He paused for effect. "Do I have a second for Mr. LaMark's motion to allow an informed tenant to address the Board?" He said "informed tenant" in a way that made the adjective/noun combination seem dubious. He sat with his gavel hovering above the sounding block, his furrowed brow daring anyone to second the motion. He smiled. "Hearing no—"

"So moved."

Crowe made a quick fist of victory in the air close to his chest. It was Mrs. Montgomery! He wondered, if while drumming up votes, LaMark had told her that the visitor would be Harvey Crowe.

"Let the record show that Mrs. Montgomery has seconded the motion," Burke said. "Discussion?" He pointed. "Director Harris."

"Who is this person? Why are we hearing from them?"

LaMark cleared his throat. "His name, to my knowledge, is Harvey Little. He would like to address the Board. He has information he feels we need to hear."

Harvey Little? Then Crowe put it together… a combination of Harvey Crowe and Chicken Little. Well played, Crowe thought, well played. The "to my knowledge" was a nice touch.

Burke pointed his gavel in LaMark's direction. "Certainly you don't mean for us to give up board time whenever a tenant would like to address us." He looked toward what Crowe guessed was the camera wall. "Of course we value tenants, but if every time—"

"Point of order," LaMark said.

Burke snapped his glare in LaMark's direction.

"Sir, in all fairness, my motion is not for every time. It's for this time, and it has been seconded."

Burke studied him as though he hoped LaMark might dissolve under his withering stare. "So it has. Is there any other discussion regarding Mr. LaMark's unorthodox request?" He surveyed the room, his head pivoting like a lighthouse beacon. "Hearing none. I will call the vote. Those in favor say 'aye.'"

The room echoed with the word. Burke determined that it was too close to call and asked for a show of hands. Eight of twelve board members were in favor. Burke made a point of speaking aloud the name of each director that had voted in the affirmative. His tone sounded as though he were listing a group of people he would like to see go to hell.

Crowe turned and one of the delivery people handed him his file folder. He turned back and set his hand on the door.

"May I call him in, Chairman Burke?" LaMark asked.

Burke nodded begrudgingly.

"Mr. Little?"

Crowe took a deep breath. Something surged through him, like a heavy liquid in his bloodstream—the weight of every life he bore. The plan had gone well so far, but the moving parts were suddenly too much for his mind. So much more had to go right. What had he been doing, tittering at the security guard's sarcastic remarks? This wasn't a prank. Was he still his old self… an obsequious coward currying favor with those who might bully him?

An image that he'd suppressed for days, even months, flipped on in his mind like the screen coming to light in a movie theater. Everything else was darkness, and there was nowhere to look save for the image. For a moment it was just the building as he had seen from drone photographs. It stood tall, cradled in the ribcage of the exoskeleton, a collection of essential concrete, rebar, and steel girders that kept them alive, giving them someplace to live away from the toxic air. It stood… and then there was a small rumble. Not the intermittent moans of the building settling, but the rumble of something starting—an ending starting. The lower floors tremored as if trying to shake off a chill. And then the fall began. The building stooped, just slightly, as though a spinal bone had slipped, a sudden but slight loss of height. A plume of dust rippled out between the first and second floors. Another ring of dust from somewhere in the middle of the floors, then answered by dust emerging from the roof. It started in slow motion—the weight of everything pressing down on load-bearing columns and walls and a foundation that could no longer bear it. And then the sinking, as though the ground had become water, the building disappearing, drowning into it, slipping through the ghost of a lifeguard's Kisbee ring, not orange and dense, but gray and dissolving, unable to buoy anything.

It played in his mind so slowly—the fall—as though taking place over years, a symbol of all the years they'd ignored the signs, rationalized their choices, and let their eyes see nothing through their cataracts of greed and denial. Implosion, falling in on itself, "the center"—as some poem he remembered reading noted—"cannot hold."

Still sinking, vanishing, and then being replaced by the pillars of dust rising around it, the structure a reluctant magician's assistant realizing that there was no sleight of hand, no illusion, no fog machine, but just the sudden knowledge that this dark magic was real, and she would be gone for good.

And then everything sped up and it was fast and so loud that all the screaming voices could not be heard over the roar. The force of it, like a ship sinking into the water, pulling the dust and debris back down with it. Until there was nothing left, just a roiling tsunami of detritus and wreckage spreading outward, its gray disappearing into the barren landscape and the unrelenting hued sky beyond.

"Mr. Crowe?" It was one of the delivery men setting a questioning hand on his shoulder. "You okay?"

Nodding, he exhaled his long breath and pushed open the doors, walking into the boardroom. The room smelled of polished wood. In the distance, the Board blurred in his vision, but he could make out their craning necks to see him. Glancing to the back of the room, he saw the broadcasting glass. It was a one-way window, a mirror on the boardroom side reflecting the semi-circle of directors. Behind it, a small broadcasting crew worked the cameras and audio equipment. The glass itself was a huge lens, an eye watching everything. In a recent board meeting, Burke had reported that viewership of their meetings had risen to nearly 70% of the building residents. Crowe hoped the numbers would be even better during his presentation.

He walked down an aisle created by the rows of wooden chairs on either side of him. The room seated nearly one hundred. Scattered throughout the room were only a handful of tenants, all very old and still. A few looked to be sleeping. One woman he passed was crocheting, and he fought the conspiratorial thought that she may have been planted in the room, simply to shake his confidence.

Harvey Crochet! Harvey Crochet! Won't put up a fight, just runs away.

A railing near the front separated a row of chairs from the rest of the gallery. He had come to board meetings in the past when more of the public had been encouraged to attend. The special seating in front, cordoned off from the rest, had once been reserved for reporters from the Building Gazette. During public comment, they would offer difficult, probing questions for the Chairman or other board members to field. The paper had been the first to report that small cracks in the lower floor apartments were increasing exponentially. Then, five years ago, the Board, in the interest of easing unnecessary expenses, had voted to eliminate the newspaper co-op fee.

"Some," Burke had said at the time, "choose not to read the paper, and should not have to pay for a service they find lacking in value." Instead, the paper would only be funded from that point forward by voluntary subscriptions. The number of reporters at the meetings quickly dwindled and, six months after the vote, the building newspaper had folded altogether.

Crowe stepped up to the podium that directly faced the Chairman's seat. Burke studied him, and Crowe saw a growing recognition in his eyes, his fingers twitching on his gavel. Crowe set his file folder on the podium top and opened it with trembling fingers. He looked at the faces staring at him, receiving tiny encouraging nods from LaMark and Montgomery. He forced a smile. A fever of heat washed over his skin.

"Ladies and gentleman of the Board," he started, "thank you for offering a concerned tenant some of your valuable time to address you. My name is Harvey Crowe, and I—"

Suddenly, Burke's gavel smashed repeatedly into the sounding block as though he were trying to bring the building down all on his own.

Crowe stopped cold. Damn it! Nervous, he'd blown it, not using the alias LaMark had offered. The entire collection of faces turned toward Burke's hammering which had cracked his sounding block in half as it went ricocheting onto the floor in front of them.

"Point of order! We were informed that this man's name was Harvey Little, and yet he introduces himself by another name? The previous motion was made and voted on under false pretenses."

The room sat silent a moment. Even Burke seemed uncertain as to what the next move should be. His eyes flared with anger and confusion. He looked toward a hand extended in the air.

"LaMark," Burke said. It sounded as though he'd spoken a profanity.

"Mr. Chairman," LaMark started. "I would also like to ask a question regarding your point of order. What does his name matter?"

"It matters!" Burke squeezed the handle of his gavel, his deep breaths swelling and deflating in his chest.

"Mr. Chairman, I would like to make a motion—," Director Peoples offered.

Burke, seemingly relieved to have the opportunity, banged his gavel onto the table in front of him. "Director Peoples, you are not recognized by the chair!"

Nodding, she smiled, and then raised her hand in a slow, theatrical flourish.

Burke stared, and then shook his head as though coming through a fog.

"Director Peoples."

She smiled again, making a show of hanging her head and averting her eyes. "Thank you, Chairman Burke, for the permission to speak, sir. I would like to humbly make a motion that in light of this astounding new information that the Board be given the opportunity to vote again as to whether or not we wish to hear from Mr. Crowe."

Crowe's heart felt frozen, his blood seeming to stop like a river finding itself in the midst of a sudden, hyperboreal winter day. This could all backfire!

"Second," LaMark said.

Burke rapped his gavel for no apparent reason. He paused, seemingly to collect the thoughts rushing into his head.

"Given my interest in this motion, I would like to step down as chair, briefly, to participate in the discussion and the vote. As you know, the chair neither participates in discussion nor votes."

"Mr. Chairman," director Peoples said, "you've participated in discussions in the past."

He nodded. "And had someone made a point of order regarding it, I would have checked myself. My passion for the operations of this building and its tenants can get the best of me. In this situation, I feel compelled to follow appropriate protocol and so hand the gavel to vice-chair Calloway."

Calloway. It was one of the names Burke had mentioned when doing his roll call of those who had voted in favor of the original motion to let Crowe speak. That would mean one less vote in favor of his speaking and one more opposed. The bastard.

Director Calloway, an elderly woman from the 96th floor, took the gavel. "Discussion?" she asked.

Burke crossed his arms.

Crowe seethed. The chairman's only intent had been to vote.

Calloway acknowledged the end of the discussion, repeated the motion, and then asked them to vote by a show of hands.

Eyes flashed around the room.

Calloway tried to suppress a smile. "And with a counting of seven hands, the ayes have it." She turned to Burke, gavel extended. "I assume you want this back."

Burke, red-faced, shook his head. "As a temporary regular member of this body, I would like to make a motion to—"

"You haven't been recognized by the chair, Mr. Burke," Mrs. Calloway said, her wrinkled lip quivering with satisfaction.

Burke looked ready to burst. After a moment, he raised his hand.

Calloway nodded at him, rapping the gavel lightly for effect.

"Thank you," Burke said, staring at his gavel in her hand. "I would like to make a motion that we limit the amount of time that our guest speaker can address the Board to three minutes in the interest of protecting the Board's time."

The double doors to the boardroom swung open the moment Burke completed his motion. Crowe turned to watch them—children flooding into the gallery, finding places in the empty seats. The tenants sleeping in their chairs were jostled awake. Many of the kids were students that he tutored and a few of them waved to him. Following them came a vision, a lady of the lake with red hair Crowe knew all too well.

He turned quickly to see Burke, his empty hand hammering with nothing, making no sound. "Mrs. Calloway," he finally said, imploring her.

Mrs. Calloway, instead of sounding the gavel, waited for the children to be seated.

Sarah stood in the aisle. She smiled.

"Madame Chairwoman, I apologize for being late. Sarah Simmons, PS20, seventh-grade history. My class is studying the workings of government right now, and this seemed like the perfect time for them to witness government in action. We are studying the history of free speech specifically and its importance to cooperative government."

"Mr. Crowe!" one of the children shouted.

Crowe blushed but stayed facing the Board.

"Well," Mrs. Calloway started, "if your pupils can maintain decorum, I see no reason why they can't stay."

Burke crossed his arms tightly, looking as though he wanted to collapse his ribcage.

"Point of personal privilege," LaMark said, stifling a grin. "Given the welcome, but unexpected arrival of our young visitors, I would ask, for my clarification, that Director Burke repeat his motion."

Without looking at the gallery, but instead directly at LaMark, Burke reluctantly repeated his motion that Crowe's speaking time be limited to three minutes.

"That's not fair! Free speech!" shouted one of the children.

"Boo!" shouted another.

Mrs. Calloway rapped the gavel. There were no more outbursts from the children. "Do I hear a second for Director Burke's motion to limit our guest's ability to speak?" She looked around the table. Most eyes were looking into their laps. "Hearing none, the motion has fallen to the floor."

Burke immediately held out his hand for the gavel, which Mrs. Calloway returned. "Before we continue," he said, "I am going to move this body into a closed session."

Some of the children grumbled in protest.

Burke sounded the gavel until the room was quiet. "We are in uncharted waters. We are about to be addressed, apparently at length, by a speaker from whom we will hear God knows what. The veracity or relevance of what he will say..." He stopped. "In short, as the Chairman, I choose to move this body into closed session given the unconventional direction the proceedings have taken." He offered a moment for the gallery to be emptied.

Crowe watched Sarah leave with the children. She glanced back over her shoulder at him, offering an encouraging though sober smile.

Burke then spoke to the air. "Broadcast control, would you please at this time terminate video and audio broadcast."

A woman's voice, unfamiliar to Crowe, spoke through a speaker mounted on the ceiling. "Affirmative. Broadcast has ceased."

Burke thanked the voice and then turned his attention to Crowe. "You may proceed."

He reopened his file, trying to hide his shaky fingers. "As I mentioned, my name is Harvey Crowe, and I would like to bring to the Board's attention some issues of accuracy regarding the load-bearing vulnerabilities of this building." He stopped and looked around the room. "I have some documents that I would like to project for the members to see."

A few board members who had voted in support of the presentation grumbled, damning LaMark with their stares. They'd likely been told that the visitor to the boardroom had positive news.

Director Peoples spoke up to tell him a camera in the podium light would project any document he set under it onto screens in front of the board members.

"Thank you," Crowe said. Though he tried, he couldn't keep his leg from shaking. "I have read the reports from the Board about the weight coming into the building versus weight leaving the building. As an example, if you will look at your screen..."

Crowe adjusted the paper under the camera while the Board turned their attention to their monitors.

"Mr. Crowe?"

He looked up into Burke's face, a portrait of fake sympathy. "Do you need a moment? Your hands are shaking. Does something about your presentation have you nervous?"

Crowe shook his head, making a note to himself to keep his hands out from under the camera. "I'm fine," he said. He pushed his fingers through his damp hair. "Here you will see is the Board's report last month for weight coming into the building versus weight leaving the building. You can see..."

"Point of inquiry, Mr. Chairman, may the Board be reminded again as to who chairs the Load Monitoring committee?"

"I do," Burke said.

Peoples smiled. "Thank you."

Burke's nostrils flared.

"You can see," Crowe continued, "that the committee's report shows 26% more weight leaving the building than coming into it." He gave them a moment to study their screens. Then, he swapped out the piece of paper for another. "Now here are numbers from last month for the scales at the Receiving Bay, the Outbound Bay, and the Refuse Bay. Here," he said, pointing at the totals, "these calculations show 38% more weight came into the building than left." He gave them a moment, listening to their muttering. "That's a substantial difference between what is reported and what is accurate."

Burke called for a point of inquiry. "Interesting. Though likely an anomaly. Now, could we see these comparisons between these two sources for the last year?"

Crowe looked at him. "I don't have that."

Burke nodded, smiling. "So, you are asking us to draw some kind of conclusion based on a discrepancy found during one month—one of the building's most volatile months I may add when high emotions could easily lead to a clerical error?" He continued by adding that in the heated labor environment, the Delivery and Maintenance Guilds could be doctoring the numbers to make the Board look bad.

"I think the Board should draw its own conclusion. I'm simply making you aware of—"

Burke nodded. "We appreciate you coming in."

Crowe put his hand on his folder. "With all due respect, I'm not finished."

"I apologize," Burke sneered. "By all means, continue to illuminate us."

A few of Burke's cronies snickered.

Crowe placed another piece of paper under the camera. "Recently, the Board touted the success of Operation Steel, which I will remind you proposed—"

"Mr. Crowe, please don't insult this body by trying to remind us of our actions. We know Operation Steel involved the installation of 20 new steel pilings to—"

"Which, Mr. Chairman, in all fairness, ended up being 10 steel pilings," Crowe said.

"A number," Director Durant chimed in, "that subsequent research showed would more than brace the building against recent load concerns."

Crowe crossed his arms. "That research is suspect."

"Mr. Crowe," Durant said, "what is your profession?"

"I was in marketing."

Durant nodded. "Word spinning. Okay. And what is your current occupation?"

Crowe crossed his arms a little tighter. "Community activist."

Durant smiled. "So, as a community agitator, you are qualified to question the research of—"

"Mr. Durant, some decorum, please," LaMark said.

"No, Director Durant," Crowe said, "I suppose I am not qualified, but here..." He set another piece of paper under the camera's eye. "This is a report that shows only four of the ten steel pilings were properly installed."

"The authors of the report?"

Crowe cleared his throat. "They are three architectural students that I can produce to walk you through their findings if—"

Durant laughed. "Architectural students? Good god. Are they going to debate with contractors and architects with far more years of experience and knowledge?" He shook his head. "Mr. Crowe, it strikes me that you are wasting the Board's time with this presentation." He put air quotes around the word.

Crowe looked at LaMark. The man's expression did not look confident. He raised his eyebrows to say, "skip this small fry stuff, go for the panic rooms."

Crowe continued by showing photographs of the cracks in the lower-floor apartments.

"All of which, if they aren't already, will be bonded even stronger with epoxy," Mr. Burke said. "I almost wish we would have left the cameras rolling since the weakness of your presentation would have served to comfort the tenants. As it has been you that's been terrorizing them for years with your pamphlets and conspiracy theories."

Crowe looked around at the faces. He was losing them. Mrs. Montgomery looked as though she might cry. "This," she was probably thinking, "this is why I ran for the Board? This is why I live in a nearly empty space?" But even with her crestfallen face, when they made eye contact, she nodded him encouragement. If they could just know the plan. He wanted then to tell her, to tell LaMark, to tell Peoples—

"Mr. Crowe," Burke said, banging his gavel. "I would like to say this has been enlightening. I would like to say that, but I'm afraid I can't."

Crowe looked down, flipped through his file folder, and looked up again. He had figures on the exoskeleton, flaws in its design, and graphs that showed its actual effect on the building's structure versus the reported effect. But then, his sources were the same architectural students.

"Mr. Crowe," Burke said, smacking his gavel harder against the table.

"The Spring Cleaning Day—"

"What about the Spring Cleaning Day, Mr. Crowe? Now you'll try to slander one of the most cooperative days this building has ever seen?"

"It was..." He shuffled through his papers. "There were... the official report said that nearly..." Sweat dripped from his brow. He dabbed it with the back of his hand. "If you will give me one moment to find—"

"Mr. Chairman," Mr. Durant said, "how much longer do we need to endure this? It's a sad spectacle at this point."

"Then panic rooms," Crowe nearly shouted, seemingly panicked himself.

Burke's attention snapped up for a moment, his eased demeanor going back to consternation.

"Indeed, I think you need one," Director Harris said to the delight of several members.

"No," Crowe said, "I have a blueprint. It's..." He flipped through his folder only to have it slip from his grip and scatter over the floor. He crouched, frantically gathering up his papers, photographs, and reports.

Burke's gavel sounded again. "Stand up, Mr. Crowe. Please."

With papers cradled in his arms, sticking out like straw from a scarecrow, he rose.

"With permission from the Board, I would like to have a moment to speak one-on-one with our guest," Burke said.

"To what end?" LaMark asked.

"To give him a chance to regroup and to ascertain what of any substance he has to share with this body. As Chairman, I have a responsibility to make certain our time is used well and to keep us focused."

LaMark crossed his arms. "I think we've heard some substance."

Burke nodded. "Within the chaos, I will agree that there were nuggets of information we should revisit." He looked around the table. "Would one of you please make the motion—"

Durant's hand shot up, and Burke acknowledged him.

"I would like to make a motion that we allow—"

"If I may," Crowe said, raising his voice.

Burke hammered his gavel, but the Board's attention was on Crowe.

"In the interest of not wasting any more of your time, I can spare you the need for discussion or voting." In his peripheral vision, he could see LaMark shaking his head. "I'm willing to speak one-one-one with Mr. Burke."

Burke nodded, grinning—like a spider in its tunneled shadows feeling the tremors of a victim lighting on his sticky web.

Crowe swallowed the ball of fear that had gathered in his throat.

CHAPTER 11

Burke clamped his heavy hand on Crowe's shoulder and guided him toward the back of the room near the one-way glass, out of earshot of the others. Crowe stared at the ground as they walked, his feet shuffling as if adjusting to walking in manacles. He looked back once, and the faces of LaMark, Montgomery, and Peoples looked as though they were watching an innocent man being escorted to the gas chamber. He felt pity for them… sorry that they had believed in him, that they didn't know.

Reaching the back, the two men stood and faced each other. Their doubles faced each other in the reflective glass. Taking in the reflection, Crowe saw the absurdity of the matchup. He stood lifelessly—already defeated with slumped shoulders and a sheen of sweat on his face—in the shadow of Burke's barrel-chested torso. He towered over Crowe standing at six foot five. Crowe wore the dated suit of another man; Burke was tailored in the latest fashion. A nauseating cologne, as though mixed with formaldehyde and chloroform, wafted from his body. Crowe's head swam with confusion in the permeated air of Burke's manufactured scent. He set his hand against the glass to steady himself, leaving a wet palm print.

Burke smiled. "Ah, the best-laid plans of mice and men, no?"

Crowe said nothing. He lifted his lolling head to keep eye contact.

"You don't look well, young man."

His wet palm slid on the glass, leaving a snail's trail. He took an unsteady step and adjusted himself. "I'm fine," he said, hardly believing the words himself.

Burke crossed his arms. "What did you hope to accomplish today?"

Crowe blinked Burke's face into focus. "To share the truth."

Burke chuckled the amusement of a man with the upper hand. "The truth? And what is the truth as you see it?"

Crowe collected himself, took his hand from the glass, and steadied himself on his two feet. "It's the same truth that you already know… that maybe not today or tomorrow or even next month, but eventually, and much sooner than anyone can imagine, this building is going to collapse into a tomb of rubble. And why? Because of the way greed kept you and certain members of the Board from making decisions that could save it. And I know you know that to be true. It's as true as you are powerful… and corrupt."

Burke laughed again. "Ah, so now you become an orator. Where was this speech-making ability only moments ago when you had our rapt attention? You seem to be the epitome of too little, too late." He laughed again.

"No, that would be you." Crowe shrugged. "And maybe I did miss my chance to make my mark, but it doesn't change the fact that what I've said is the truth. People are going to die because of you and your grifting. I just want to hear you admit it to me… to yourself."

Burke scoffed. "You are a puny and insignificant man. You had your fifteen minutes, and you spent them stuttering and stammering."

"Then why not let me finish? Why not let me crash and burn, and through my incompetence demonstrate once and for all that there is nothing but conspiracy and unfounded fear behind my claims… our claims? Why did you want to talk to me one-on-one?"

Burke uncrossed his arms and rubbed his palms against each other. "Perhaps it was kindness. Perhaps under my loathing for you I found pity. I wanted to give you an opportunity to leave here with some dignity. I wanted to encourage you to come back to the podium, apologize for wasting our time, and then commend the Board for its efforts to make this the best place to live—"

Now Crowe laughed—loud enough that the other board members sat up. His laughter bellowed from within him like something finally released from a cage, like the wolves from the documentary he'd watched, their fierce eyes and restless pacing, still haunted by the wilderness they once knew like a phantom limb.

"So finally," Burke said, raising his voice above Crowe's fireworks of sound, "your lunacy made plain by your pathetic soundtrack. I offered you dignity, and you choose dishonor."

Crowe's laughter idled down. Still, he smiled menacingly at Burke. "'The best place to live?' You can't be serious. Have you bought into your propaganda? Have you been to the lower floors? Have you seen the filth and squalor those tenants live in? The scraping to get by? The corpses in the stairwells and hallways? The dirty water that runs from the faucets like the liquid from the rotting carcass of the building—"

"You can stop your litany now. Nobody is listening. Certainly not me."

Crowe pointed at his chest. "The dismal lives lived down there are a direct result of the Board's actions and inactions. You say you brought me back here to offer me dignity, but that is something you don't know how to give. You've bowed your head at the throne of power, greed, money, and a certain perverse self-preservation for so long that you can no longer lift your eyes to see that for most people it is a kingdom of struggling, lies, and despair."

Burke crossed his arms again, his neck reddening. "I offered you a chance, but like every time life has offered you a chance, you've blown it. I will let the Board know that you have concluded your presentation." He made as though to turn away.

"And what if I haven't?"

Burke turned back. He studied Crowe's face for a moment before reaching slowly, deliberately, and touching his cold finger to the ghost of a bruise on his cheek. "I think you're done… Chicken Licken."

Crowe nodded his head in understanding. "So those men who came to my apartment to silence me… to beat me up because I'd finally chiseled some pennies from your mountain of wealth… you sent them?"

Burke smiled. "'Throne of money'? 'Mountain of wealth'? You are quite the maker of metaphors, mixed as they may be. Yours is 'The folly of mistaking a metaphor for a proof.' But, in answer to your question, yes. And if I am forced to send them back, they won't be gentle this time." He turned on his vindicated heel to return to join the others.

"You are afraid," Crowe said to his departing back.

Burke stopped, turned, and walked back to him. "You have more to say."

"You offered to talk to me one-on-one because I explained that I was prepared to discuss the panic rooms next. The mention of them has you panicked."

Burke laughed.

"Admit it."

"I don't know what you're talking about."

Crowe smiled. "I have blueprints. I have witnesses."

Burke walked towards him and kept walking until Crowe's back was pressed against the glass. Crowe could feel two Burkes—the one in front of him, face flushed with anger, and his doppelganger behind Crowe reflected in the glass.

"And what do you think would happen... I mean, if the Board even believed you? Do you think they would vote to dismantle the panic rooms? Stop construction? Would they vote to take away a feeling of security that many of the tenants crave? Do you think the Board would vote to enforce load codes and forcibly remove tenant's belongings?" He pointed his finger in Crowe's face. "This board votes the way I want them to vote, and if they don't, I find ways to get the people I represent what they want."

Crowe swallowed, looking at the manicured nail of Burke's fingertip. "You represent the entire building. This is a co-op."

Burke shook his head. "You seriously think I care about any one of the bottom dwellers in this place? The thieves and degenerates? Do you think the captains of ships stayed up late at night worrying about the people in steerage? The stowaways?" He smiled. "See, I can make pretty metaphors too, Mr. Crowe."

Crowe crossed his arms. "I've seen the future."

"You are insane."

He cleared the thick mucus from his throat. "I've seen the schematics for Operation Landing Eagle."

Burke stared at him, his face showing a small crack in its arrogant confidence. "That's a contingency plan—"

"But it's your plan. Rather than enforce the load limitations now, you'd put your faith in a preposterous zero-hour strategy? The fact a plan like that even exists is proof that you know what could happen to the building." Crowe nodded. "Worried now aren't you…that's the way your face should look."

Burke said nothing.

"The blood's draining from your cheeks, Mr. Burke. Now it's you that doesn't seem well."

Burke's pointing hand fell to his side.

Crowe began describing aloud to anyone in earshot the image of Operation Landing Eagle. The 100th floor is being repurposed as an impact and stabilizing floor. The 101st floor is being refurbished to contain the building's boilers, electrical grid, and central plumbing… a mechanized maintenance crew. The exoskeleton will morph into something like an elevator shaft with suspension cables attached to strategic locations to slowly lower the topmost floors down onto the wreckage of the collapsed lower floors.

"But something the blueprints don't show—the deaths of everyone on the 99th floor and lower." He shook his head. "You imagine the upper floors just dropping into place like… like what, Burke, angels from the clouds? Somehow ready to function on top of a mass grave? The efficacy—"

"Are you quite finished?"

"No." Crowe pointed at him. "I'll be finished once I've had the chance to explain your master plan to the rest of the Board—to show them the prototype images."

They were schematics he knew that he did not have. Dagmar had only been able to dig up whispers of Operation Landing Eagle. He was repeating only what he'd heard, not what he could prove. But Burke's expression told him that it was all close to the truth.

"That's enough." Burke stood, a statue, except for the flickering of his left nostril. "You honestly think anyone will believe you—that I'll grant you that chance?" He shook his head, smiling with malice. "No, you're about to be expelled from this meeting. Your body will be found in the morning, another victim of bottom-dweller crime. Your files will find their way into an incinerator." Then, he nodded slowly. "And as to any of your allies, they will meet a fate similar to yours, including that spikey-haired bitch."

Crowe felt his cheeks flushing.

"Ah, now *your* face changes. You care about that filthy minx, don't you?"

Crowe spoke through clenched teeth. "She's a friend."

"Then I'll be sure to see to it that she gets special treatment." Burke waited. Then he laughed. "What, are you finally at a loss for words, Chicken Licken?"

Crowe sucked his teeth as his mouth filled with saliva.

"I'm giving you the chance to get in the last—"

With a sudden explosion, Crowe spat into Burke's face.

Members of the Board stood up from their seats. Durant started towards them. "You all right, Chairman Burke?"

Burke's hand shot into his coat pocket. It came out again as quickly.

Click!

He was holding a switchblade. Crowe's arms raised instinctually, but instead of stabbing him, Burke chopped with his other hand at Crowe's forearm. Then, he dropped the knife clattering to the floor.

"He has a knife!" Burke shouted, kicking the blade some several feet away.

"I didn't—"

Durant hollered for security. Two men slammed through the double doors, weaved through seats, and threw Crowe up against the broadcast glass.

Durant stood at Burke's side, looking at Crowe pinned against the wall and then looking at the knife. "Good show, old man," he said, putting his hand on Burke's shoulder.

"I suppose I'm always ready for something like that," Burke said, using his sleeve to wipe the spit from his face.

"Mr. Burke?" a woman's voice came over the room's speaker. "Mr. Burke?"

Even with his face pressed up against the glass by the two security guards, Crowe smiled.

Burke jolted, stepped a few feet back, and looked toward the ceiling. "Y… yes?"

"You should remember to smile." It was Dagmar's voice, weak but enjoying itself. "You're on camera… and coming in loud and clear. Bitch."

CHAPTER 12

Wearing a respirator, Crowe stood in the Outbound Bay, looking at it framed in the oval of his lenses. It was after eleven o'clock at night, but the semi-trailers were still being loaded. A truck flapped out through the plastic drapery of doors. Another pulled in behind it and onto the scale. Standing in the unloading dock, Crowe was surrounded by chairs, televisions, statues, boxes of books, sectional couches, an electric organ, two hot tubs, a single slate pool table, an armoire, a baby grand piano, a weight set, and at least three safes. Delivery personnel were bringing more in, filling the bay nearly as quickly as it was emptied. Over the last three weeks, Load Evaluators had visited every apartment above the 40th floor to set weight limits and to offer weight estimates for various items. Tenants had two days to choose what to offload, and whatever remained had to fall within the code. The lower floors would be visited in time, but the bulk of load infractions were known to be on the upper floors. Watching the trucks come and go, Crowe thought of Dagmar.

She had been an essential part of the plan that fateful night. While the delivery people that had come with Crowe to the boardroom entrance had distracted the security guards with talk of the upcoming negotiations, Dagmar and a contingent of ACT members had seized control of the Board's broadcasting room. "Without hurting anyone," she later reported to him, smiling condescendingly through what was still obvious pain. He'd advised her against leading the operation. Since being brutalized, she'd operated with the deliberate movements of someone with chronic pain. When asked, she always gave the same answer: "I'm fine." She'd worn a ski mask, not to protect her identity, but to keep anyone from seeing the face that now shamed her.

As a result of her contributions, the conversation between Crowe and Burke had been broadcast to the entire building with 76% viewership. Before Burke could gather his gavel and other papers, the boardroom was stormed by tenants from various floors calling for his resignation. The other board members were confused until they were escorted into the broadcasting room to watch a recording. When they returned, they voted unanimously to oust Burke and replace him with Mrs. Calloway as interim chair. After spending an hour in a security holding room, Crowe was released to go back to the boardroom. Without explanation, three other board members resigned. Emergency board members were voted in, which included Harvey Crowe and Sarah Simmons.

The meeting had continued long into the night and the next morning. Food and beverages were brought in to fuel the work ahead. Crowe was able to finish his presentation, and the precarious state of the building was made plain. Motions were offered, seconded, and voted on. Immediately, before the meeting had ended, all luxury deliveries were suspended. The trucks that came into the bay, the delivery personnel searched through them for grocery deliveries, and then sent the rest back down the ramp to the automated factories and warehouses. They also voted that in the coming days the panic rooms that were out of compliance would be demolished. Tenants could still reserve the right to build a panic room that fell within the code that the Board had originally established.

Even as the Board worked towards what would be the next steps to saving the building, tenants of their own accord began bringing items to the Refuse and Outgoing bays. Trucks came rumbling through that first night and the tenants loaded them on their own. Tenants from the lower floors came to the bays to find items they needed: bedding, dishes, furniture, and the occasional entertainment items. They risked having to give up those items when the Load Inspectors started on the lower floors, but it was generally understood that they owned less and would likely fall well within the load limit for their spaces.

Other tenants, a mix of people from various floors, found Burke. There the vigilantes brought him to the Refuse Bay and formally banished him to the outside. Crowe suspected that other board members and tenants were equally guilty, but Burke's final action may have been his most honorable. He gave up no names. Still, the Board had already voted that there would be investigations on every remaining member when their more immediate work subsided.

Burke pleaded that his family knew nothing of his actions as the chair. He asked that they not be punished with banishment for his sins. Pushed out alone onto the service ramp, he trudged down to his certain death at the ground below. He would either be knocked off by one of the trucks or if he was lucky, descend down to the ground level to slowly die somewhere outside the protection of the building. There would be nothing else for him but the toxic air and the ravagers. All the automated factories were miles from the building.

Years ago, a group of bottom dwellers with stolen ventilators and patchworked hazmat suits had left the building to seize one of the mechanized grocery farms. They never returned. Some entertained the thought that they had started their own community called One For All, but most laughed it off as pure fantasy.

There were tenants who believed that there were other buildings out there in other cities. On certain nights some had even picked up the rare radio signal. Voices, indecipherable but there, spoke briefly—ghostly— into the darkness, crackling with static.

In the loading bay, Crowe pulled off his respirator. The condensation of his sweat and breath cooled his face. He waved to a few familiar people and then left the Outbound Bay. He'd had a dinner meeting on the upper floors and told Sarah that he'd spend one more night in his apartment so as not to wake her when he returned. Although she said that she didn't mind being woken, he'd insisted. He wanted a night to himself to turn things over in his head. In the three weeks since Burke's ouster, the building was already so changed, so much better. But it left him wondering too what he would do next. He had devoted years of his life to the cause—to ACT. Now, he was giving more and more thought to Sarah's suggestion that he teach. She had a point. He was good with the kids, and he enjoyed the work. He could go back to being a part of the building's schools. Living with her, he wouldn't have the burden of rent to get him started. He nodded. He could do it. He really could if he wanted.

But then was his work done? Would it ever be done? Flashes of that evening's dinner came back to him as he walked down the stairwell.

He'd sat at an ornate table with Mr. Coldwater and several of his associates with interests in the automated factories. The apartment was on the 146th floor. The other men drank from tumblers of ice and whiskey while Crowe sipped at a glass of water, wanting to keep his wits about him. He made a mental note to send the Load Inspectors to Coldwater's apartment again as it looked ripe with load infractions. There were rumors that some of the inspectors were being bought off with bribes.

Already, he'd thought. Corruption. It's happening already.

Coldwater watched Crowe's wandering gaze. He smiled. "I see that you are looking around. I was able to get an extension on my decisions," he said. "You have to understand, much of what I own are family heirlooms." He smiled. "Has the Board looked at our proposal for load cap trading?"

It was a complicated scheme where tenants who wanted to own more could purchase unused load from those living on the lower floors or elsewhere. "Those people could use the money," Coldwater said. "It's a win-win." To Crowe and a few others on the Board, it looked like a slippery slope greased with greed and privilege.

"It hasn't come forward yet," Crowe said.

Coldwater smiled again. "I'm sure a motion will be made soon."

He smiled weakly and took a sip of his water.

"It would seem," Mr. Coldwater continued, "that it might be time to assess the results of the load reduction thus far. Given the successes, it might be time to allow some deliveries. Some have off-loaded more than their share and are looking to make some purchases with their remaining load credits."

"I don't think I've heard anything like that," Crowe said, though he had.

"Well, as you like to say, 'It's the truth.'"

Crowe attempted another smile and then sipped his water.

"I wanted to ask," Coldwater started, "has the Board's ad hoc investigation turned up any concrete evidence to verify that Operation Landing Eagle was anything more than a folk tale?"

"That committee hasn't reported yet."

Mr. Coldwater set his glass down. "You've become quite the folk hero yourself."

He shrugged.

"It's true. You've also gone a long time without. That doesn't seem fair, especially at the outset of a love affair."

And here it comes, Crowe thought. "Honestly, I don't want for much… other than to leave. Thank you for the meal."

Coldwater smiled. "People have short memories, Mr. Crowe. You'll need more than your fifteen minutes of fame to keep your board seat. I have access to excellent campaign managers—for you or whomever."

Crowe stood. "Elections are a ways off yet. I'm just going to concentrate on the work the Board needs to do now."

"Seasoned politicians know that they are always running for the seat they already hold," Coldwater said. He drained his glass down to the ice.

Crowe opened the door to the apartment. "I'm not a politician." He looked around the space. "I'll be sure the Load Inspectors get in touch soon once you've mourned your heirlooms."

The men looked at him as though a gnat buzzing around their ears.

"If I'm not mistaken, Mr. Crowe, you were voted in to take Mr. Durant's seat. That comes up for election in less than six months."

Crowe closed the door. There were no goodbyes.

He shook his head at the memory. It was a stark reminder that it could all come back. Bribes, loopholes, veiled threats, planted board members. And for what? So a few could sit on their treasures like dragons? A hoard they could not possibly spend, and them not knowing that the mountain they basked in is a volcano ready to erupt?

He couldn't get complacent—couldn't believe that by sweeping out Burke, they'd swept out corruption. He was only a symbol, not the source. He imagined Burke's choice not to call out his accomplices came with the promise that his family would be well cared for. How was it that such people had a great love for their own families, but nobody else?

Even with his life with Sarah coming together, his thoughts drifted regularly, but not longingly, toward Dagmar. They'd found her in one of the maintenance passageways behind the walls. The jagged end of a broken rib had punctured her lung, collapsing it. Like Leo, she'd died alone in her home. He learned what he'd often suspected; Dagmar didn't have an apartment in the building but had slept where she could. The building had a vast, largely unseen structure of maintenance-access tunnels and wall cavities. The way maintenance personnel talked, hundreds lived there. That too, Crowe thought, that is something that needs to be addressed.

He'd brought up the subject in private with an older board member to test the waters and see what kind of sympathy he might find. The board member wondered out loud if maybe these uncounted people living in the walls "like cockroaches" weren't the real source of live load issues. Crowe had quickly changed the subject.

Living the way she lived was how Dagmar knew so much. She'd crawled and climbed through the unseen passageways behind the walls. Just as how Crowe was privy to the private life of the super and his wife through his vent, Dagmar had found ways to eavesdrop on Burke and other board members. Covered in dust and grease, clinging to pipes, she'd pressed her ear to vulnerable gaps. She'd picked up bits and pieces. She strung together the story of Operation Landing Eagle, not from any blueprints that she could hold, but from what she could hear through the chinks in ceiling light fixtures. She had experts, most of them college students, but much of what she'd gathered came from her intra-wall spying. None of what they'd accomplished, Crowe knew, would have been possible without her. She'd given her life to save a building that had abandoned her to live like a rodent in its unspeakable spaces. She'd told him that she was climbing out of a cold air duct into the stairwell when her attackers found her. Remembering his beating, he shuddered at the thought of her later beatings.

The Board did make great strides in righting some of the building's inequities. Sending a plumber from the maintenance department, they learned that the freshwater cistern was fed by an artesian well that had long-ago been discovered under the building. Water was gathered in a tank in the basement and then was pumped up to the 101st floor making it available to the higher floors. With this new information, the Board voted to abandon the higher cistern and build a new one at the basement level. The water would then be made accessible throughout the building. Restrictors would be installed on all faucets to provide for fair distribution, contrary to the overuse that the upper floors had enjoyed.

When Crowe came to the fire door for his floor, he took a breath, thinking of the recent successes and the challenges ahead. He thought too of Dagmar and mourned that she'd seen little of the changes her actions had helped to bring about.

CHAPTER 13

Crowe put his key in the lock of his door. The little he owned was packed up into boxes to be moved to Sarah's the next day. The small rooms were empty. His bedframe, like the rest of his furniture, was gone, sent off to the Refuse Ramp. He kept the mattress, thinking that in the morning he would leave it in the hallway. Maybe someone who lived like Dagmar would find a use for it. He would spend one more night on it. He lay down in his clothes—his blankets were gone too—and readied himself for a period of meditation, reflection, celebration, and hopefulness. And eventually, sleep.

Sounds echoed in the foundation like the mysterious moaning from under ice-covered lakes he'd seen on old documentaries—the brick and metal of the building adjusting itself to the gradual, but steady weight reduction. The titanic building, like Atlas out from under the celestial sphere, was getting a needed reprieve.

He closed his eyes and tried to allow himself a moment of solace, but it was Coldwater's cocksure smile that met him in his mind. He was correct that Crowe would likely face a difficult reelection. More than likely, even with his notoriety, he would lose. Crowe hadn't missed the whispers already going around the building. Some called the Board tyrannical with the way they seemed to be taking away people's rights. For many, Crowe was at the heart of the tyranny.

Coldwater was also right about Operation Landing Eagle. The Board had formed an ad hoc committee to search for any physical evidence that would support Burke's video confession. They'd found nothing. And, here again, Coldwater was correct. Without any real evidence, the story of Operation Landing Eagle would become a folk tale—too evil in its intent to have ever actually existed as a contingency plan. Perhaps it had been a fantasy of Burke's in his darkest moments, but the man was gone and with him, most would conclude, any danger of such a callous plan being put into motion. Burke had become the symbol of any cancer that might be in the building, and, with his banishment, most didn't feel compelled to consider the existence or sources of other possible malignancies.

Crowe sat up suddenly and then slowly lay down again. A memorial, he thought. They could have a memorial for Dagmar. Everything had been moving so quickly when her body was discovered. With the Board working 16-hour days, there'd been no time for a funeral. She deserved more to acknowledge her death beyond a perfunctory autopsy and incineration. Given the role she'd played in saving the building, he wondered if perhaps a service in her memory might not be broadcast. She'd earned that much, and people needed to know about her. He could use his eulogy to not only memorialize her but to emphasize to the tenants the challenges that still lie ahead. "We can best honor her sacrifice," he began, whispering into the darkness, "by continuing our due diligence regarding the building and each other." He smiled and closed his eyes, working over in his mind what else he might say about her.

"Anya, wake up, I have something for you."

Crowe slammed his fist into the mattress. Again with the idiots.

"What is this? What are you putting in my hand you over-sexed pig! Get it away from me."

Crowe stood up out of bed and grabbed the edge of the mattress. He'd drag it into the kitchen and sleep there.

The super laughed hollowly. "It's not what you think, Anya. Has my flesh ever been that firm for you?" He laughed again. "I just can't live with you any longer!"

"I feel the same, Sam. I despise everything about you!"

"Your hate is a danger to me!"

"As yours is to me!"

Crowe flipped the mattress on its side and started pulling it through his bedroom doorway into the hallway. "Just kill each other already, for god's sake," he thought. He yanked on the uncooperative mattress.

"Do you see this, Anya?"

"What is that? What do you have?"

"Dynamite, Anya. A whole box of demolition dynamite."

A cold sweat washed over Crowe. No, he thought.

"You'll kill us both! It's madness! But then so be it. Give me my stick back…oh happy dagger!"

Crowe bolted from his apartment, down the hallway, and to the stairwell. He descended, the words in his head echoing the rhythm of his pounding heart: "No. No. No. No. No."

He ran past filth, past needles, past bottles of liquor. Past bodies, maybe asleep, maybe dead. Past graffiti… all of it denoting anger, despair, hatred.

Arriving at the lowest level, he reached a fire door locked tight. He pulled on it, threw his shoulder into it, and then stopped and just listened. He heard or imagined he heard or hoped that he heard them still arguing, bickering, threatening. If they just kept talking… maybe it was all just talk.

He collapsed against the door, his fist pounding it like Burke's gavel.

"Love each other," he shouted. "Just love each other!"

Again and again and again.

In time, his voice lost its volume and went raspy. His fist went still and he fell against the cold metal.

"Why can't you love each other?" he asked, near sobbing. "Just love each other."

The words left his mouth a whisper. A prayer. The same one as always.

AUTHOR BIO

Jeff Vande Zande teaches fiction writing, screenwriting, and film production at Delta College in Michigan. His award-winning short films have been accepted over 200 times in national and international film festivals. His books of fiction include the story collections *Emergency Stopping* (Bottom Dog Press) and *Threatened Species* (Whistling Shade Press). His novels include *Into the Desperate Country* (March Street Press), *Landscape with Fragmented Figures* (Bottom Dog Press), *American Poet* (Bottom Dog Press) and *Detroit Muscle* (Whistling Shade Press). In 2012, *American Poet* won a Michigan Notable Book Award from the Library of Michigan. In 2020, Whistling Shade Press released his new collection, *The Neighborhood Division: Stories*. He maintains a blog at www.authorjeffvandezande.blogspot.com.

Made in the USA
Columbia, SC
17 October 2022

69565863R00124